VEIL

—— *of* ——

SECRECY

MARGARET FRANCESCHINI

PAGE PUBLISHING, INC.
New York, NY

First originally published by Page Publishing, Inc. 2019

ISBN 978-1-64544-080-2 (Paperback)
ISBN 978-1-64544-081-9 (Digital)

Printed in the United States of America

To Russell, at only twelve years old, you spoke God's words to me as you brought my attention to the life living inside me when you said: "Mom, there's a person living inside a person."

To Russell, Gilda, and Adam, I whispered to you from the beginning of your creation, as God breathed life into your beings, you are my precious gifts,

To the lives that were unjustly taken away leaving their mother's womb vacant, and to those who were lifted away from their mothers arms to be allowed to live a new life.

And to my husband who I left for hours in the day to hide away and complete this book, thank you for your support and encouragement during this challenge in my life.

CHAPTER 1

Her tears puddled onto the old photo, fading the image as though it had been left out in the rain, washing away the memory of the past and its veil of secrecy.

—MF

Everyone makes misjudgments, and any young girl in any town across the world could have an inaccuracy of emotions. After all, trust when it comes to love, and a belief in love dissolving all boundaries, is all part of the innocence of youth.

A life-changing event for one young girl manifested in the modest fishing town of Twillingate, Newfoundland, on the northeast coast of the Atlantic Ocean in Canada. A tiny population occupied this small province, which linked to a vast corridor of ocean running down from Greenland.

Julie Gagnon was turning sixteen this June, and she was not one to spend her time with the young crowd, drinking their nights away in the old woodshed by the creek. She felt far more mature than the reckless boys who made suggestive advances toward her, and instead, she preferred reading in her spare time and taking nightly walks to the end of the road where she could witness the sky melding into the sea and the sea meeting the land.

She sat on the damp driftwood, listening to the uninterrupted sound of the waves calling to her in perfect measure. The scent of the sea and the breeze embraced her body and mind, encouraging her to write poetry and then, with eyes closed, making her nightly wish.

"The sea is my friend, so I send out my wish to the waves who will carry my dream out where adventure and a new life is waiting for me. I have to travel and taste what the world has to offer me."

Her town, with its tiny cobblestone streets and narrow pathways, was all she had ever known. A town, which seemed separated from the rest of the world, almost like a castle surrounded by a moat of the sea.

It was 1950; no one locked their doors, and there was nothing to fear. Life was simple living in Twillingate yet hard-earned work for the fisherman, as Julie came to understand as she watched her parents working at the local fish market. "This town has been my cocoon all my life, since I have turned sixteen last June, and this is a new year, I have earned my independence. I can make my own decisions as an adult. I look forward to finishing high school and my employment at the bakery then moving onto my journey into college." A summer breeze passed around her, she giggled and thought. *At least now, I can drink black coffee with father!*

"Dad, we work too much. With my workload at the bakery and yours at the fishing company, we barely spend any time together."

Her father sat back, adding sugar to his black coffee as his nightly treat.

"Well, Julie, it pays to work from morning to dusk. We surely have enough money for food, so you should be thankful for that." He sounded tired.

Logan was born and raised in Canada, with a long family history of fisherman. He resembled his ancestors with his short and stout stature. He held a firm belief that hard work and perseverance gave rewards.

"Julie, you have to work as hard as a fish pulling on the line if you want success."

Julie nodded. These were her father's same words to her each day, his eyes always flashing concern as he attempted to prepare his daughter for life's challenges.

"I know. I am saving all my money so I can go to college. And look at the strength I inherited from you. Maybe I am that fish pulling on the line."

He gave her a sudden strange look and then she burst out laughing. He joined in with a hearty chuckle. She admired her father and his reputation as the generous man. He always brought home some of the daily catch after it was weighed at the buyer's market, sharing whatever he could with his neighbors.

"Dad, I'm going to need to hear a man's point of view when it comes to me dating, so I'm glad we talk the way we do. Oh, and by the way, I'm still waiting for your approval of my future husband."

"Well, I hate to tell you that the young boys of my generation in comparison to the youth of today is the same when it comes to maturing. Guess I'll have to mail order a husband for you."

Julie laughed. "No thanks, Dad. I think I'll just wait. When I go off to college, that's when I'll meet him."

"Beware, darling, men are natural hunters, so be wise to their craftiness. Don't be too quick to give yourself away. My dear, I know how busy you are with work and your studies, but you are known to keep to yourself. You very much have my personality, but you remain very solitude from the other teenagers in this town. Don't you miss getting out now and then?"

"Dad, don't worry so much about that. If people are saying such things, then maybe they are jealous that I am thinking ahead for my future. I am perfectly happy with my writing and studies. Hanging out will just deter my ambitions. Being alone with my thoughts in my solitude is my comfort zone. So let them label me an introvert. I'm happy."

Their tiny white cottage held a small kitchen where her mom made sure everything was sparkling clean, and Julie laughed at the way her delicately built mother growled out orders in the kitchen like a pit bull.

Emma, also born and raised in Canada, met Logan while in high school, where they became sweethearts from the start. She was a vibrant, enthusiastic, and feisty woman who used her culinary talents to make her fish dinners tastier than any professionally chef's. Julie had to smile as her mother's tone became stern as she explained how she made her preparation for the food.

"Mom, are you an executive chef of the highest rank?"

"Listen to me, young lady. A confident woman always wins in life, and especially an argument, so you've got to be strong."

There was a remarkable resemblance between mother and daughter, in both their facial structure and their striking long wavy red hair.

"I see myself in your piercing blue eyes. Be careful who you catch with them."

"Oh, Mom, you and Dad seem to like to compare me with a fish all the time. But I am very glad that I resemble your pretty looks, but I hope with my feet on the ground I will measure over your height."

They both burst into peals of laughter.

That evening, Julie walked to the sea as she usually did. She sat listening to the music of the waves crashing against the rocks. Thinking back to her childhood, she remembered always returning to this one quiet place where thoughts and words consumed her mind, and she wrote it all down into her memo book.

Watching the flicker of the lamps on the fishing boats tied to the small wooden docks, she could almost taste the sea. The scent of fish still lingered in the air as she gazed upward to the twinkling stars winking like watchful eyes. A shooting star flew overhead. Even the seagull's cries were silenced as a canopy of darkness enveloped the sky.

She said her wish aloud, "I promise to pursue my education in creative writing, possibly work as a journalist. Maybe if the waves froze over, I could skate across and escape this little town and never return."

The next day at the bakery, the usual customers kept her busy with orders of fresh hot rolls and breads. She was fourteen when she started working at the bakery with an early thought of saving her money and looking ahead to college. The townsfolk were delighted, knowing she had the personality to stay home and not associate with the troubled teens from her class. Julie was regarded as the most skilled baker of the best homemade pastries in town.

Butter tarts, sugar pies, and raisin cinnamon breads filled the bakery with a distinctive fragrance. She learned everything from the head baker, Frank, who taught her the puff pastry technique of folding the dough with the butter, making it remarkably flaky. The town orders for Julie increased for this delicacy prepared especially by her.

She matured from fourteen to sixteen, and being with Frank the Baker so often she began to feel an attraction to him. She found herself glancing over at her boss, examining his dark wavy hair and trim, muscular body. She felt shaken whenever she spoke to him, even if just about the orders of business. She felt as though his deep, dark, coffee-brown eyes penetrated her soul, and she had to look away.

It has been almost three years since I started working with him. At first, I thought it was just a teen crush, but now I realize I am very attracted to him and feel very serious about him. Julie's thoughts about Frank continually ran through her mind.

A white Christmas had ended as January's new year brought a change in Julie's life. When the other workers left, she worked to close up the store, secure the locks and lower the electricity before leaving.

As she went to get her coat from the back room, she saw him sitting behind his desk, counting the money made for the day. When he saw her enter, he stopped. They both stopped and, with their eyes fixed longingly on each other, forgetting everything else, slowly walked toward each other as if in a daze until they were wrapped in each other's arms. Julie couldn't resist the feeling of his arms around her body, his strength, and an overwhelming desire to want more of him. Her lips brushed up against his strong shoulder as she inhaled his masculine scent. She embraced him firmly, feeling his body heat pulling her toward him. Slowly her breaths turned to moans of pleasure calling his name.

As he gazed into her eyes, he became enraptured, caressing the warmth of her body's supple curves. With his lips covering her mouth, he felt a burning tension as he gripped her frantically and sank into her sweet cry of joy.

This unexpected union felt endless, filled with every sensation, but as always happens, time eventually worked its magic, making the memory fragile and faded.

In the cool of the early morning the next day, there was a hush between them. They hid their relationship from all the customers, not wanting any secret to be known to their little town. But after-hours, the onset of the night belonged to them.

Weeks passed, turning into months, as they held their clandestine meetings at the closing of the store. Their relationship grew stronger with the changing seasons.

"This feels so magical. Life is so mysterious how it brought you to me. You have made my days exhilarating, my existence romantic. It's made me uninhibited. I feel like I can write with a freedom I didn't have. I now write in such a different way."

Julie breathes softly one night lying next to Frank with deep contentment.

"I have never seen red hair like yours, and your blue eyes melts my heart each time you look up at me. I wait for you each morning to see your smile, and it brightens the start of my day. And when I'm home, all I do is think of you. You drive me mad."

Frank turned his gaze to her in a tender way, assuring her of their love.

Every time they met, their parting was more difficult, having to go their separate ways, but with a promise to each other that they will meet the following night. Julie retreated to the sea and sat with thoughts swimming in her head as she began to write little notes to him.

Frank met his wife at the culinary school of Montréal. They graduated in the same class then married that year. She was offered a job a few towns away from Twillingate, whereas Frank wanted to remain in his small town. He had the opportunity to open up his own bakery, which was his dream. Life seemed pleasant for Frank to live and work in his own town. His wife was comfortable working out of town with a popular bakery and under the direction of a fine chef.

Next morning, he arrived earlier than the workers and found the note on his desk.

As he began reading, he found himself feeling weak, leaning on his desk for support, then thinking and shaking his head. He thought, *I feel so torn by my deep love for Julie, yet I love my wife of five years. Julie is so vibrant, witty, and strikingly beautiful to my eyes. She has invigorated my life. Although my wife has a beauty of her own, she is calming and so opposite in personality. I have never cheated on my wife before, but this feels like I'm supposed to be with Julie.*

With winter passing and taking with it a cold chill and snow, Valentine's Day approached, bringing love in the air.

"I have planned a discreet Valentine's dinner in the back of the bakery for us, so we will close a little earlier than usual, especially since our customers have all made earlier purchases for this holiday. Then we can spend our time of celebration."

Frank lovingly said to Julie as he sneaked a kiss behind her neck.

"Of course, you did. I already expected that from you, so no surprise. I just don't know exactly what the surprise is, so that will be interesting. Then again, you do have a romantic, passionate heart."

She whispered in a mild voice as she swept pass him with a little dance in her steps.

That evening, once she locked the store doors, she entered the backroom, shutting and locking the main door behind her. A sweet fragrance of lavender flowers greeted her as she walked into the dimly lit room. The candles scattered around, presenting a luminescence of golden hues outlining her subdued, unsteady silhouette on the wooden floor.

"You hopeless romantic arranging all this for me? I can smell a mixture of lavender and roses, but I can't distinguish the scent of food you cooked."

Her voice rose with eagerness as her heart continued with an intense beat.

"Oh yes, your little nose found the pleasant smells like perfume. You have sharp senses. Just follow the trail of rose petals and wonder where it will lead you."

He replied with yearning as he peered over the corner of the wall.

As she turned the corner of the small room, she found rose petals arranged all around the dinner table set for two. With the sound of laughter filling the room, they sat, enjoying their dinner. As he served her his special dessert, she found a note under her plate, and in his scribbled handwriting, she read aloud.

"Breathe the words of love that keep me singing, spoken words that keep us clinging."

"Oh, Frank, I am amazed at your writing. You really know me. You have given me a little treasure. It may be a little note, but to me, it is valuable, a masterpiece that I will hide in my basket of notes I have in my room."

As she gave his hand a loving stroke of thanks, their eyes connected; and in the ambiance of the candlelit room, they moved to a more intense and passionate tone of love, driving their feelings to a euphonic state of elated ecstasy.

In that late evening as the candles grew dim, she was stirred by the dancing shadows on the wall.

Resting her head on his chest, she uttered in a strained voice, "Looks like nightfall is ending our time of bliss. We have to separate now, so I'll hide our notes. There are no names on them, so if found, no one will know it's us. Someday I'll combine these notes into a book of poems. I hope I make it to college someday. I need to prepare for my future."

His fingers kneaded her shoulders while exhaling a hard breath.

"You will go to college and leave this town. You're smart, and you will live your dream. I was born and raised here and never had the ambition to leave and start a new life somewhere else. But you have that opportunity, not that I want to lose you, this I do not want, but what is more important for you at such a young age? You have to follow your dream."

"Oh, Frank, I don't want to lose you either, but there is really not a good college in this area for what I am looking for. So I have to go somewhere else, like New York City. Maybe by then you will come with me."

"My Julie, time will tell us what to do. As for these notes, you know I can't take any of our notes home, but I carry it in my heart. I'll be thinking of you all night now. It's a little late, and I have to get home, and so do you. I'll see you in the morning."

Julie wrestled with the guilt of their secret meetings. There were times that she thought of her long talks with her father and felt a heaviness on her chest. A confession was always on her mind but definitely out of the question. Her hope was that by the time she was eighteen, she could tell her parents and maybe marry and leave with Frank. Only her silent thoughts rested in her mind for now.

In late April, she noticed a little weight gain, not thinking much about it as she tried to button her skirt. She heard that sometime during the teenage years, the menstrual could stop because of some kind of hormonal imbalance. So she made her appointment to visit to her family doctor. She mentioned to her parents that she would be going to see him since she felt very tired and hoped he would give her a vitamin.

Dr. Palmer sat back on his black leather chair, pulling on the gray beard covering his chin, and with his furrowed brown eyes narrowed on her, he strongly spoke.

"My dear Julie, I brought you into the world. You are like a daughter to me. Now, I need to know who is the father?" His strong words were followed by his hand hitting down on his desk.

"Oh, Doctor, I had a feeling I was pregnant but didn't want to face it. I can't talk about the father. It is very complicated, but please just help me."

Julie sat in the soft, brown chair opposite his desk with her hands holding her head and tears flowing like a never-ending river.

The gloom of the moment crept into Dr. Palmer's heart as he rose from his desk and sat in the chair next to her. Holding one of her hands and trying to ease the feelings of distress she was going through, then he spoke gently to her.

"Julie, I am responsible for your medical condition, and I have been a family member for years. It is my obligation to alert your parents. But before I call them, I want you to go home and talk to them. I will help in this situation. I already have an idea in mind. Don't be troubled. There are always changes in our lifetime. This is a tremendous change for you, but I promise you, it may look bleak now, but it will all work out."

With a somber look in her eyes, she sat with slumped shoulders and a feeling of wilting away.

She then answered her doctor, holding on to the chair with a tear-streaked face, "There is a life living inside me, and it is part of him. I am carrying his child, but I'm a child myself! I'm so scared right now. I want to keep the baby, but I can't stay in this town. This is not a town, it's a little village with no sympathy."

"This is why, my dear Julie, I need to approach the father next. First, go ahead and talk to your parents. Tell them to call me, and we will have a family session. Then I will go to his parents and straighten this out."

That night, instead of going straight home, she went to the bakery, knowing Frank was still there, preparing for the next morning. She went to the back door since the bakery was closed and gave it a secret tap for him to know that it was she.

"What a surprise. I didn't know you would see me tonight. You can help me get these things done. What excuse did you tell your parents so you can come here tonight?"

Dreading telling him the news of her pregnancy and not knowing how he will react, she searched his eyes as she spoke while her arms wrapped around her waist to steady herself.

"Frank, I saw my family doctor to night, and he confirmed that I am pregnant."

The eyes she once knew as deep, dark, and mysterious became as one falling into the depth of the abyss.

With his teeth clenched, he grabbed her wrists, shaking her violently and screaming, "I did not hide the fact that I am married. I told you from the beginning, as for children I never wanted. I cannot divorce her, this I explained to you. All this year I thought you were on birth control, protecting yourself and me! You have to go back to your doctor and ask for the new injection that will help you to pass the pregnancy easily. It's so early into your month, and no one will know about it."

Astonished at his words, she felt her face flush with heat and anger, twisting her wrists to unwind in his hard grip.

"Let go of me. You're hurting me. Why are you acting like this? I never saw you in this way before. How could you be so coldhearted? All our secret meetings, you said you loved me like no other. You lied to me!"

As he pushed her off in disgust, she slammed against the wall next to the door. For a moment she was frozen in time.

Like an earthquake quivering under her feet then running upward in her body, she ran outside, slamming the door behind her. Leaning against the closed door, listening and hoping for him to come after her, waiting through the deafening silence with the only sound of her pounding heartbeat, feeling abandoned with tears streaming down her face, she found her hands slowly following the tears reaching down to her swollen belly. And with a soft touch to the small roundness, she knew abortion was not the answer. Just the thought of part of her and part of him becoming whole and living inside her, she could never terminate this life. Feeling so alone and depressed, she went home and cried uncontrollably, telling her parents of her pregnancy and how violent the situation turned.

"Julie, we spoke on previous conversations about dating and believing boys' lies. Tell me which boy from this town were you with? I will go to his parents. He will not get away with physically hurting you. After I speak to his parents, I will get in touch with our doctor."

He sat down next to her on their sofa, shaking his head in dismay of this unexpected news. Then with a shaking body, he began to walk toward the door.

Clenching her father's hand and pulling him back, she choked out her words frantically to him, "*No!* Dad, I can't talk about it. Please don't be persistent. Doctor said he has a plan, so please, I beg you. I'll go away. I'll go anywhere, just please, let's not talk about the father, not now, but I promise you at the right time, I will tell you the truth."

At that point, as her parents saw the pasty, washed-out look in her face, they decided to just hold her and comfort her. They huddled together in tears; her parents pledged to make sure she would be safe.

As this stressful situation rose with so many unanswered questions sending them into a tailspin, their thoughts turned to their trustworthy anchor, their doctor and dearest friend who they knew will have a rational answer for this situation.

The next morning, they all arrived at the doctor's office. He greeted them with compassion and helped them to settled down and listen to what he had planned.

"I am so sorry you have to go through this torment with Julie. I love her as my daughter. That is why I am going to help you. I am in contact with friends and the nuns who manage and operate at a convent called The Fold. Some of my colleagues knew of a few girls outside of this town who had made the same mistake and, once enrolled, were able to continue their education after surrendering their babies. I believe The Fold is the most notable for her and will set her on a path to a distinguished career. I will make the appointment for all of you to visit The Fold. Julie will register to live there during her pregnancy, and she will have to sign legal documents for adopting out her baby as well as your signatures, since she is a minor, parents' signatures will also be required. We three have stated our position on this situation. Your parents have turned to me for your well-being. Julie, this is the best choice for you and the baby."

The parents agreed to this arrangement and returned home with Julie and began to help her pack a few things. Blackness engulfed Julie's thoughts as she followed the instructions of her parents. Tiredness like a creeping sorrow grew over her body, leaving her cold and numb.

That evening as Julie and her parents sat in their backyard, a purple spring-season night sky was nicely viewed. Trying to see the beauty of dusk while discussing all that transpired at the doctor's office, her father noticed tears flowing down her cheeks with her head bowed and knew it was a sign of depression. He gently lifted her chin in an effort to console her and, with his small white handkerchief, dabbed her tears with soft strokes.

"Julie, we have talked before about life. I taught you to always trust us and come to us. Life is full of wounds. This one we are all living together. It has varying effects for all of us, including the unborn child. As you know about our discussion with the doctor and the decision we agreed with, the call was made, and we have an appointment next week to enroll you at The Fold, where you will be safe and well taken care of."

Emma spoke with meaningful eye contact on Julie; being a strong woman, she tried to put on a brave face while holding so much emotion in her heart.

"We are so sorry, but we cannot afford to take care of you and a child. As much as it hurts us to suggest this, but you have to give up the baby for adoption. You have a whole life ahead of you, and your dreams of becoming a journalist will not come true if you stay here. Please believe us that we feel a deep pain in our hearts about giving up our grandchild. We are not concerned that the gossip of this small town would hurt us. Our concern lies with you, but most importantly, the town's verbal abuse to the child. Julie, you never know, someday we may meet your child, and it will be at the right time in all our lives."

Julie consented with a nod of her head, but for a moment, the thought was expelled from her mind, still wishing to keep her child. Yet her thoughts turned to the reality of knowing that there was no other way. Feeling fatigued, she went to her room to be alone and just think of the extreme changes happening to her life. In her tiny bathroom, leaning against the small porcelain sink with its pink wall mirror, she looked at her red tear-streaked face. She saw the red marks on her wrists from his violent grip and the redolent of his breathe from his screaming so close in her face. She decided to bathe and scrub off his scent and his final touch.

Like a spider molting the layers of my skin, I'm washing away memories of your fingerprints you left behind. My heart cries out like the pang of pain, watching it fall into a narrow pit; it's leading into the darkness of a bottomless ocean, where there is no sight.

CHAPTER 2

The following week, they made their long travel to the south-eastern coast of Nova Scotia, Canada, where The Fold was located.

Logan took out his old map of his country, Canada, and proudly waved it to his family and called them to the table where he laid it out for them to see his plan.

"Here we are this little spot on the map is Twillingate, we will follow this route for six hours until we get to St. Christopher's Hotel in Port aux Basques harbor."

Their eyes followed his finger along the blue line, which was the route he explained.

Great outline Dear, I am glad you are in control of this because I would not know what to do without you. Emma's eyes gleamed at her husband.

Logan continued with his outline of their travel as he pointed to the next part of their trip.

"I think that would be enough time in the car for all of us, especially Julie. We can stay there for the night and after an early breakfast continue on our route to Nova Scotia. We have to take a ferry, with the car, to the other side and land in Sydney. From there we will drive another... Logan's conversation was broken by Julie's questions.

"Dad, how far is this trip since we have to take a ferry?"

Logan not lifting his eyes to Julie and with a reddened face answers.

"Honey, it's about nineteen hours to get to The Fold from Twilligate. It is really a very secluded old pavilion on the Atlantic Ocean. I am sorry, but this is the best answer for us all. We will make plenty of overnight stays for your resting. Please bear with me, this is the most important decision we had to make for you."

All Julie could think about was how tired she felt and hoped it would not be a very uncomfortable ride.

"Julie, I know what you are thinking, but it will not be uncomfortable. We will take care of you all the way there. Dad has everything planned. We will stay overnight at different places for your rest and for your dinners. Once we get there you will understand why our doctor chose this place."

"Its okay Mom and Dad, I'm just a little nervous, but with you I know I will get through this."

They made plenty of stops along the way and in the nicest places to sleep for Julie's comfort and to eat the best meals for her nutrition.

The following week, they made their long travel to the southeastern coast of Nova Scotia, Canada, where The Fold was located. Because of its location and being the second-smallest province, it gave Julie the feeling of being like a hollow in a wall or a niche. Her first glimpse was quite a spectacular sight as she gazed at the grand, old, white-painted pavilion, with the sun deck filled with white wood rocking chairs bringing out strong images of its past. The foyer was flooded with natural light from windows that reached from the old ceiling to the floor. It was elegantly decorated with antiques and a tastefully plush carpet in the greeting room. Marble side tables with antique lamps and alabaster marble fireplace brought warmth to the room. Most of the young girls already with living arrangements greeted her and her parents with kindness, helping them to feel comfortable and at ease. A voice from the distant room that sounded like a soldier giving orders appeared.

"Let me introduce myself. I'm Ms. Stella, the director of this old establishment. Please follow me to my residence across from the pavilion, where we can all privately make the arrangements. We all want to extend to you a comfortable time of relaxing with tea and homemade muffins. We understand you have taken a long journey to get here, so we will return to our living room when we are done with the paperwork."

Following a path of round pavers leading to the director's little white cottage where she resided just off the main road, there were flower boxes that were attached to the cottage windows with overflowing purple and pink impatiens flowers and vines dropping to the ground. Julie took in a breath and could taste the flavor of the sea, as if she was still at home in Twillingate.

"This is my office and my private living arrangement, also where future adoptive parents will come to sign papers and take the child. You will sign these papers, giving permission to The Fold to have adoptive parents take your child. These arrangements are made here privately."

She then turned to Julie's parents, giving them more information about what to expect at The Fold.

"We have a hospital staff on the premise. When we get back to the pavilion, I will introduce you to our midwife who also has living arrangements at The Fold. Her assistant is Sister Grace who is our staff nurse, also Nurse Lee who is a recent graduate to our staff. I also have a degree in nursing and in business. All of our nuns are skilled and certified in teaching the high-school level. We are in the process of having a medical doctor on staff in the very near future. In the meantime, the town hospital is about twenty minutes away, not too far in case of emergencies, which we never had to use. So you see, we are very organized. Julie will blossom here. No need to worry."

Far from disheveled, her tailored white crisp outfit matched her strong personality. Her posture seemed to have a strong willpower yet graceful as a ballet dancer. She sat upright and rigid like a sergeant major as she handed over her desk papers to be signed.

Julie felt a dark cloud over herself and, in a state of extreme apprehension, took the pen with an involuntary shake, placed her other hand over the pen to have control, then signed the document.

"I know this is a difficult time in your life Julie, and just as difficult for your parents. I see that together you are such a supportive family for each other. We all experience setbacks in life's journeys. We are here to help you to move forward and give you time to process what happened. Let's go back to the pavilion now. You must need to sit and rest. The girls made a special recipe for you to taste. And it will be good for you all to get to know the girls and maybe hear their stories, so you, as parents, can understand."

There was a tone of warmth, or maybe compassion, as she guided them out her door. Interestingly, she now appeared like a person under twenty-five, her white cap covering most of her hair with just a glimpse of some soft blond curls sneaking out the sides of her cap.

After comfortable seating on an old, stuffed Victorian sofa and some treats, Julie's parents listened to some of the stories a couple of girls shared with them.

"My name is Nancy, and I just want you to know that right now you feel the same as my parents did when they brought me here. But they left with hope for me, and now that I am due for my birthing, I have finished most of my education. I will be ready to go home soon and begin my college studies."

"This is difficult for us, but you have just given me hope for my daughter, that she also will finish her education and move onto a good profession."

Emma found it difficult to talk to a stranger yet felt she received some strength to get through this.

"Well, young lady, it is time to leave and check into the bed and breakfast down the road so we could get a head start early in the morning."

Julie's parents thought it best to leave at that point because they didn't want to see her room. They felt they already struggled with having to leave her behind. Finally, they were able to retreat to their car, sitting with slumped shoulders and both sighing and having a fast pulse in their throat. They felt such emotional pain for their daughter and the grandchild they will never see. As they drove down the road, it felt like a deep, dark tunnel, which brought out their uncontrollable cries.

"The warmth I once felt in my heart is now replaced with pain. This heaviness in my body feels as if I'm in mourning," Emma cried as she leaned on Logan's shoulder.

"I know, dear, you used the words that describe my feelings. We will never feel the same again. We may never see our grandchild. Something that we both wanted in our elder years has been erased from our lives."

"Yes, Logan, but at least Julie will be cared for and move onto college next year," Emma whispered to Logan with a little hope in her voice.

That afternoon was filled with introductions for Julie. She was taken to her own room by one of the young girls who helped her to unpack her suitcase and hang up some clothes.

"Julie, so glad to meet you, I'm Susan. I have been living here since June when I was only a few weeks pregnant. My baby is due in February, so my parents thought it would be better to continue my studies here until the baby comes, then they want me to come home. It has been an emotional time for me, but I am so busy with my studies and with the counseling sessions it has helped with the depressed thoughts. Also, all this has helped me to prepare for the future adoptive parents. Sounds like I'm happy about it. Believe me, it took all these months of preparation to come to this point."

"Thank you so much. All this sharing has given me a feeling of acceptance here, and everyone's support is making this transition so much easier. Just when my life seems so bleak and everything looks at its worst, your voices seem to change my heart for the good and for my own benefit."

"Oh, Julie, I became involved with an older man also. He stole my heart and my life. It was a muddled affair that left me in a mental state of confusion. We all have a different story, we all share your pain, but we are here to push on to a more favorable outcome. Trust me, you will make it through this condition."

Her eyes went glossy as she fought back tears explaining her story to Julie.

"Oh, Susan, you do understand. He would penetrate into my soul with his dark, solemn eyes and use skillful words, enchanting my mind as he whispered words I never heard before. I was young and now believe that our affair was all a smoke screen, a ruse, a deception. He disguised his real intentions as I gave myself away to him."

The words in her mind again began forming a verse: *A final remark to me you gave, before your final breath, when I heard your last words of anger. You made me a new path, and it washes over me like the ocean clangor.*

"We have all been in a similar situation, Julie. That's why we are now here! I thought I was deeply in love with my man. He was older and wiser, and he knew exactly what he was doing. I was young and stupid, so here I am. But this is where I belong, and I know for sure this is the right thing to do for my baby."

Her reassuring words helped Julie accept this temporary fate and to believe she can move onto a better life.

Each new day was another day for building emotional strength for Julie as she kept herself busy at The Fold with all the recipes she stored away in her memory. But the memory of Frank the Baker kidnapped her mind with his dashing, chiseled face and trim, muscular body. She was able to finally share her memories of Frank and her experience with his deceit.

It was November 20, 1950, and she was busy making her homemade pumpkin pies and specialty breads for everyone at The Fold. It must have been all that standing and mixing ingredients, all the bending over and stretching to take out the pies from the oven, which must have brought on her labor. She felt a fierce pain shoot across her belly and grabbed onto the tabletop, screaming for help; the piercing cry brought everyone out of their rooms as the nuns and midwife came running in to assist her.

"We do not have time to get her to the downtown hospital. Bring her to the rear part of the house into our small medical room where we can prepare her for birthing."

The midwife and nuns hovered over her in deep concentration and, with compassion, were watchful that no problem arises with the birth. Julie noticed the gray walls around her and the sterile smell of disinfectant. The overhead fluorescent lighting blurred her vision as her muscles tightened with each oncoming contraction. She took deep breaths and felt her legs press hard against the metal stirrups.

The midwife's warm voice tried to put Julie at ease as the painful intensity grew, while one of the nuns standing by wiped the sweat from her brow with a cool cloth.

"Okay, Julie, you're doing fine. When you're ready, I'll help you up to push."

With each painful push, she gritted her teeth and cursed the name of Frank loudly. Her breaths came in as stabbing gasps when her eyes shifted to the clock on the wall. She started timing her contractions, watching the hands of the clock ticking away, and thinking all the time spent in her life has brought her to this point, so alone in a distressful suffering.

The labor became stronger, more intense, the pain deeper to the core, and with each painful push and each piercing scream, she saw the hands of the clock move closer to twelve. The merciless, repetitive pain forced the birth with a final agonized scream searing through her body, and at the stroke of midnight, her baby girl was born.

All the birthing pain was gone with the sound of the newborn's first cry and in unison with Julie's own sobs pouring gently onto the infant as she held her in her arms.

"Yes, little one, your cries bring you to a new, unknown life. I'll name you Cinderella, for midnight brings a new day and new beginning for you."

She brought her close to her lips and gave her a soft kiss, taking in a breath of the fresh scent of her baby, and held her against her chest as a cascade of tears spilled onto the infant.

With a painfully piercing heart, Julie spoke to her newborn in soft whispers, "Through my tears, you will have my motherly scent. It will always stay with you, and through it, you will someday know me. I will never nurse you or watch you grow, but someday we will meet again in another time. My heart will not heal until I see you again."

After cleaning and wrapping up the baby in a warm blanket, the nuns asked Julie if she would like a picture of the newborn to keep so she can always look back at the moment of her baby's birth. So with an old Polaroid camera, Cinderella had her first photograph. As Julie's new infant slept by her side, she wrote her a note:

> *When you were taken out of my life, your soul still remains a part of me; my dreams of you will bleed like a never-ending river, yet mended by the visual memory of you, held in the basin of my heart forever.*

As they fell asleep, the tears vanished, but their breathing became synchronized and their heartbeats in the same rhythm as the timing in a melody.

The next morning Julie looked out her window and saw a young couple arrive at the cottage. Squinting to see what the couple looked like, she only saw a dark-brown hat covering the woman's head and dark-brown wavy hair on the man, giving Julie a vision of Frank's dark-brown wavy hair and a terrible memory. Split emotions came over Julie with guilt of the decision to hand the baby over, sadness already missing what just lived inside her. She felt loss and emptiness all at once as she held her daughter for the last time. She knew she had to turn Cinderella over to the couple siting there in the director's cottage. She remembered the director said there was to be no contact between the new parents and the birthing mother, but she knew somehow, she had to give them a note for Cindy in hopes that someday she will read and know the truth.

In the cottage, the director explained to the couple why the birth certificate has the name of Cinderella.

"We are curious why she is named Cinderella?"

"Well, as the story goes, just like Cinderella, at the stroke of midnight, she was born, so Cinderella seems appropriate to the mother."

"We love the story and agree it seems appropriate, but as you know, we have to change her name to keep this personal and secretive."

The director agreed and sent Nurse Lee, to Julie's room for the baby. As the nurse came into the room, she inched forward, extending her arms to Julie. She looked up with an empty stare, knowing it was time to hand over her daughter. She took one long hard breath of the infant's scent and, with a lack of energy, handed her over.

The nurse held the baby with a dulled expression and, trying to be a comforting person, spoke quietly to Julie, "You are definitely making the right decision since you are so young. They will raise her and give her a beautiful life. I know how you feel, since I had a miscarriage, and it also felt like I gave up my baby. I know and understand the emotional pain you feel. I am so sorry you have to go through this, but remember, your choice will make a difference in her life."

Julie's face went blank, and a flush crept up, revealing a strained silence in the room. Then she handed the nurse an envelope with a large C written on the front.

"Will you take this note and give it to them to read to her when she comes of age. I hope to go to college and become a writer. This will be my first note to her. I will save the rest, hoping to see her again one day."

"I understand. I will have to ask for permission from the director first. From there we will see what comes of it. Please don't get your hopes too high."

The nurse took the sealed note with the baby and, with a quick turn, left her room.

The director met the nurse and the baby in the outer office and agreed to speak to the couple.

"I have a sealed note here from the mother requesting that you save it for when the baby comes to age, or if you decide to ever tell her about the adoption."

"We see no harm in this and will certainly keep it until we believe it is time to reveal the truth. We understand what the mother is going through. You can tell her we accept it."

The nurse then walked in with the baby all swaddled in pink and handed her over to her new parents. Their eyes glistened at the sight of her beauty, and with a grateful thank you, they hurried to the car.

Julie listened to the crunch of gravel as the car drove away; she wondered if anyone would enter her life with love and understanding and pierce this veil of secrecy surrounding her traumatic surrender of her child. She lay still and numb for a long time, with arms crossed cradling the photograph, as if cradling her child. She could still smell the scent of her baby as it lingered in the room. Languishing in an injured mental state with exhaustion taking over her body, she could still hear the echoes of her baby's first cries faintly leave as she drifted into a sleep of depression.

That night when the couple finally returned home, they willingly kept the note hidden in one of their files. It remained in the back of the filing cabinet for years, untouched and forgotten. They believed that when it was time to tell Cinderella about the adoption, they would open the note together. In the meantime, they already had a lawyer draw up papers, changing the baby's birth name to Marina Cynthia. They thought that since the baby was born near the sea, Marina would be suitable, and Cynthia would take the place of Cinderella.

CHAPTER 3

I t was a chilly morning of November 20, 1966, when Marina Cynthia looked out her big picture window. She loved the view of the New York skyline amid tall buildings where she lived in her Manhattan luxury apartment. This was where her parents brought her home sixteen years ago and the only life she has ever known. Not wanting to venture anywhere else, she thought how convenient it was to live here in Manhattan, and so close to her cousin Laurie living just around the corner. Both were at the age of sixteen and almost sisters, but no resemblance with Marina Cynthia's big blue eyes and long flowing red hair tied up with purple berets. Laurie had a short brown bob haircut and large brown eyes wide open, always filled with excitement. Marina Cynthia and Laurie anticipated their Saturday mornings where they sat in Marina's bedroom and shared their secret girl talk.

Marina sat and daydreamed about what to write next for one of her poems, while Laurie was always the first one to start a conversation about the boys in their classes. The room was warm and cozy with lilac Swiss dotted curtains falling softly to the floor, allowing the sunshine to peek in. They loved sitting on Marina's big, full-size bed surrounded with large pillows in an assortment of colors, talking and laughing as they sat on the cushiony, soft pink comforter with lilac seams running through.

"*Little paper notes—that's what love is like,*" flicking some of them into the air and watching them spinning down onto the purple carpet, the childlike Marina said to Laurie.

Laurie, being so amused by this analogy, all she could do was laugh.

"Paper only fades and rips just like doomed relationships. And you're such a daydreamer, so no, Marina! There are no little love notes to believe in."

Laurie enjoyed making funny faces at her by pressing her hands into her cheeks.

"Well, someday I will use my daydreaming thoughts and write about it! It will be love letters like the poets of past. That's how they expressed their love. Written with deep expression, kept for eternity for others to read."

Marina threw her hands up, stretching into the air and swinging her head back in a dramatic scene.

"Okay. Dream on," replied Laurie, "but not in this day. And you have to stop all this romanticism. It's gone with the 1800s. So stop sitting in your room writing love letters to the air and get out there and date. We are sixteen now and can meet some hot guys!" Laurie snapped her fingers in Marina's face while she danced around her bed.

"Friday night we are joining the senior get-together at the art museum on Fifth Avenue. I'll come get you at seven o'clock after dinner."

"Sure, Laurie, anything you say, but hey, don't forget my birthday cake tonight."

"Silly girl, how could I forget? I'm bringing my birthday present to you, and I wouldn't miss that homemade cake your mother makes every year."

Whirling around to the door, she started tossing her hair, pretending to be a model; and with several quick blinks of her long dark eyelashes, she left the room to head home.

Marina said yes then shook her head and gave a dismissive wave of her hand just to get her cousin to stop annoying her. Then she went back to her daydreaming and writing little love notes to the air. She often wondered why all these words and phrases of poetry kept entering her mind.

She thought, *Mom and Dad never wrote poetry and never cared to. I always think that something is hidden in my life, but I just don't know how to find it. Maybe it's this gift I inherited from someone in our family that lived so long ago. Someday I will search our name and find them, but right now I'll write about something hidden, like my gift of writing secret love poetry to a man I haven't met yet. Ah, a veil of secrecy!*

That night the family gathered together for Marina's home-made birthday cake.

Laurie's parents attended, bringing gifts and lots of stories and conversation.

"Uncle Louis, you are so filled with interesting stories. I think my writing gift comes from you. Certainly not from Dad who is always thinking about antiques," she said with a giggle.

"Okay, Marina. Dad's gift is finding all these valuable antiques. Mine is baking!" Marina's mother said with a quick thought.

"Oh yeah, Aunt Margaret, I wish I could bake up a cake like this. It's delicious!" said Laurie, licking her lips after a big spoonful.

"Well, I have to admit to you, Marina. Your mother is the best in cooking and baking, and I hope you have that gift also."

Richard said with a sly smirk and a wink to Marina.

The evening was over, and Laurie and her parents left to go home. Then Marina, tired and full of the birthday cake, went to her room.

Richard and Margaret retired to their room and, in hushed voices, expressed their feelings about Marina.

"Richard, Marina always talks about her gift and hoping to find her lineage to her writing gift."

"Yes, I'm aware of this, Margaret. I thought she would grow out of it by now."

"Do you think we have to tell her soon?" Margaret said with fear in her eyes.

"No, I'm not ready for that explanation to her. Let her become more mature. She still acts like a child," Richard answered, laughing.

At last, Friday arrived, and Marina, and her cousin Laurie met with all their class friends. The art museum was like a maze, tunnels of exhibits in every direction. This was Marina's first visit to the museum, which sent her mind reeling trying to comprehend it all. She stood in awe as her eyes took in all of the art spanning all cultures and time periods through all the exhibits on display. She started walking along, enjoying and imaging her life living there in 1870 when the structure was built. As she examined the walls with the intricate shapes, she began writing about the romance of grandiose hall and meeting a prince there.

Her thoughts of fantasy were interrupted, and she was abruptly startled by a voice.

"Excuse me, excuse me, young girl, can I help? You look lost."

As she made a quick turn, her eyes met with deep, dark-brown eyes of a young man, maybe in his late twenty years of age, and she felt an immediate attraction for him.

"Oh, I'm sorry. I didn't hear you at first. I did lose my friends, as I have a habit of wandering off with my thoughts." Her eyes flashed as she touched the side of her mouth while tilting her head, giving him a soft gaze.

His mouth curved into a very sweet smile, and he fumbled his words at the unexpected response she gave him, "Well, I can help. What entrance did you access? Was it Eighty-Second Street? If so, you're not too far away from your friends."

"Yes, we entered the great hall, that's when I separated but didn't realize it. I have a habit of following my imagination," she said with a mischievous look on her face.

Amused by her, he then took out a map of the museum and showed her that she walked into the gallery of 155-Greek art; with the map, he guided her to the entrance. As they walked, he explained the different wings of the museum.

"I never imagined there would be so much to view at this museum. How is it that you know every square inch of this building?" she replied as she made a circular motion around them with her finger.

"Well, I'm the art curator, so I have to know the entire structure," he said, waving the map in her face and playfully giving her head a tap with it as he gave out a note of laughter in his voice.

She found herself gazing in his chestnut-colored eyes, returning a flash of her long dark lashes.

"Very interesting, but where would you go to college for that? Probably out of state, right?"

Indicating a no with a nod of his head, he shortened his strides to walk by her side.

"I attended my four years at NYU Institute of Fine Arts and graduated with a degree in fine arts. I also did my internship here at the museum, and at graduation, I was offered this job. I'll never leave here. This is my life."

He stood with both hands tucked under his arms and one holding on to the map.

"I applied for Hunter College. I'll be working on my MFA— creative writing. I want to write novels and maybe someday edit in journalism. Since I live here in the city, and this school is rated number one, it all works out for me."

She showed him a satisfied and impressive smile as she held on to her notebooks, staring absently up at him.

"That's a great school. I'm glad you chose to go there. If there is anything I can do, let me know."

He handed her his business card and wrote on the back his name and phone number. Finally, with lots of walking, they arrived at the entrance where the others were already on their way in the opposite direction.

With his mind set on her, he lost track of time. He began quickly walking backward through the crowd, as if playing football, shouting out to her and not wanting to take his eyes off her.

"Hey, wait a minute, what's your name?"

While cupping her hands to her mouth to answer over the mixed sounds of voices echoing through the room, she yelled out.

"*Marina Cynthia*," she shouted as her name echoed against the walls.

Laurie's mouth dropped open, and her eyes flung wide as she watched him running and stumbling away.

"Wow. Who's the cute man? I mean, really handsome and so tall."

Marina's face flushed, and a nervous laugh gave away her embarrassment, as if everyone could see she already was intrigued with him. As she watched him stumble away, she knew he was different from the high-school losers and anticipated seeing him again. Was it his maturity and knowledge, or the way he looked at her with his chestnut-colored eyes that fascinated her?

"Oh, he's the curator of this museum, and he took the time to guide me through some exhibitions as he walked me back to where I lost you. He is very well informed of this entire museum and taught me some facts about different galleries and interpreting particular meanings of each one," she replied to Laurie, trying to hide her inward feelings for him.

After their trip to the museum, they all went out to dinner and shared about all they had seen, but Marina's thoughts kept returning to him and how in charge and knowledgeable he was. Between the conversations with Laurie and their friends, she had continuous thoughts of him. Then she remembered the card he gave her. She took out his card and flipped it over to see his name and saw his scribbled handwriting, Jeff, followed by his phone number. Just looking at his handwriting gave her a thrilling feeling that went through her body. This new feeling made the heat rise in her face, where she hoped to mask her new inner feeling.

After a few days of thinking about him and wondering what she should do, she felt enough courage to give him a call. Nervously dialing the phone in her room, she felt her heartbeat was louder than the dial tone. When she heard his voice say hello, her hands became so sweaty she was afraid the phone would slip out of her hand.

"Hi. Its Marina. We met at the Museum. I hope I'm not calling at a wrong time. I was about to leave you a message."

"Oh yes, of course, I remember. You were lost in section 155. This is great that you remembered to call me. I was actually thinking of you and hoping that you would. I just happen to stop at home for a break but have to get back to the museum. Let's set a date and time to meet again. How's this Friday at around 3:00 p.m. since this is my early day? Usually I work later during the week," he eagerly suggested.

"Yes, that is a perfect time for me, right after I get out of school. It should only take about ten minutes to get there. I am really looking forward to another tour with you."

As she hung up the phone, for a moment she knew meeting him was wrong and did not want to tell her parents, but she couldn't help this feeling deep inside her heart.

That Friday was the beginning of their continuous Friday meetings, always at 3:00 p.m. They walked through another different section of the museum. As they walked and he explained about the exhibit, she wrote what she saw and felt.

"You know, we have been meeting and touring the museum for about a month now. I think it's time we stopped rushing and went to dinner afterward. That would give us more time to talk about each exhibit, and you can rewrite some of your notes, so what do you think?"

He turned to her with hands held out and shrugged shoulders, waiting for her answer.

With a darting glance and a little coquettish smile, she acknowledged his question.

"That is what I was hoping for. We need more time to talk, and I usually get hungry when we are finished with all the walking and talking."

The following Friday, she explained to her parents that she would be meeting with friends and going out to dinner with them.

"That's great, Marina, I'm glad you're getting out more instead of sitting in your room and writing. Not that I feel you should stop your writing. It will definitely help with your admission to college," Marina's mother spoke with enthusiasm.

"Yes, Marina, it's good to follow through with your writing but also to get out with friends," her father proudly stated to her.

Marina felt a pang of guilt as she got ready to leave for her date with Jeff. As she reached her elevator to get to her lobby, she felt the mixed emotions of lying to her parents, but the emotions and excitement of meeting Jeff overruled those thoughts.

Jeff took her to the historical tour of the Michelangelo exhibit, where they viewed more than two hundred works. After their discussion about Michelangelo, Jeff took her to the Central Park Boathouse for dinner. Being seated by the open doors with a view of the water and the shimmering lights reflecting off the lake, she felt like a princess. The cool breeze brought with it an unknown fragrance from the lake, where she suddenly had a feeling of familiarity. She felt a little light-headedness as she watched the shining water, and feeling a little strange, she jokingly said she was going to the powder room.

She sat and gathered herself together and wondered why she felt so strange looking at the lake. Being distracted by the beauty of the ladies' room, she enjoyed its Victorian sofas and large, ornate mirrors. She thought her dad would love all this eighteenth-century furniture, then she felt guilty of where she was and afraid of telling her parents that she was with an older man. She didn't want to hurt them, since they had such a nice, trusting parent-child relationship. But after a few minutes, she felt she was able to return to her table, not wanting to keep Jeff waiting and looking forward to their dinner together.

They sat nestled in the center of Central Park with a view of the gondolas floating on the lake, listening to the soothing music playing in the background. The soft candle lighting and shimmering reflections of the moon on the waters brought their gaze to each other, and a new feeling began. As their dinner was served, Cindy noticed a pink piece of paper under her wineglass.

"Jeff, what is this paper with one of my favorite colors? It wasn't here before."

His fingers began tapping the table with a little embarrassment as he replied, "I slipped it under the wineglass when you were in the ladies' room. I really hope you don't mind."

She gently opened it, noticing his particular style of writing, and read it aloud.

It was simple, just three words were written on the note.

"Of the sea. Why did you write, 'Of the sea'?"

"Your skin glows by the lights reflecting on the lake, so I'm pretending we are sitting by the sea. Did you know your name means, of the sea?"

Flushed by his words, she sipped the wine to become calm and stared into his dark eyes.

"Yes, I know my name means, of the sea. My mother said she just loves the sea and the ocean, so that's why she named me Marina. By the way, I have a habit of writing little notes. I can't believe you do the same!"

He reddened in his face then changed the subject to a historical moment where they sat.

"Well, since I watch you constantly writing about everything you see and jotting it in your notebook, I figured you would like a little note. By the way, let me give you some history about this lake. It was originally created as a small pond in the nineteenth century. It also had a glass house and ornamental flower garden. As you can now see that over the years, it has grown and expanded for many to enjoy."

Absorbed by his intelligence and all the information he contained, Marina felt that he was even more alluring. She listened to him speak with such comprehension, her eyes following each word from his lips and searching into his dark eyes and wavy dark hair where he mesmerized her.

CHAPTER 4

Their meetings began to flow easily to more than once a week; their conversations grew longer, and their time together extended. Each time they met, it was at their favorite place, the boathouse at Central Park. The waiter remembered them each Friday and always made sure to seat them by the open French doors overlooking the lake. Bewildered, Marina always would have a peculiar feeling; there was something strange about the lake. She was almost drawn to it but eventually was able to just shrug it off.

This one particular night after dinner as they took a stroll through Central Park, in the dim light of the lamppost, Jeff took her in his arms and gently placed a kiss on her lips. She weakened in his arms and returned the kiss; they became locked in a passionate embrace.

"I have never felt this way before, this feeling that overtakes my body and mind since I met you. It is so new to me. I can't even concentrate in school," she expressed to him as she held his shoulders.

He gently pulled at her chin, bringing her closer, breathing on her forehead and taking breaths along the side of her face and into her ear.

"If I touch your smile, will I pass over the boundary? I'm so consumed by you I fumble on my words at work. I'm waiting each day for the next until I see you again," he answered her softly while still holding her by her waist.

"What are we going to do? I can't concentrate at school. How will we go on? I have to see you more often." Her voice sounded more desperate as she now clung to him, and her body knitted closer to his.

"I know, Marina. You have taken control of my mind. We will have to figure a time to meet, but not where you would be missing as much, and your parents would suspect. This Friday let's skip the museum and dinner at the park. Just come to my place. I will have dinner arranged so we can be alone for a longer amount of time. We need our private time of sharing our lives."

Since Jeff lived 632 East Eighty-Seventh Street overlooking the East River just a few blocks from central park, and she lived with her parents at 325 East Eighty-Second Street overlooking Central Park, it would not be far for them to travel and meet. Marina felt a little uneasy about lying to her parents about all the night meetings with Jeff. She knew they trusted her, especially when she was with her cousin Laurie or with the basketball meetings. But she knew they would not allow her to date an older man, even though she did not think he was that much older than her. Her feelings for him were so strong she could not ignore the fact that she was in love with him.

It was early, just four o'clock, when she entered the elevator of Jeff's apartment building. With her heart racing, she knew this night was something that would be her moment of sharing her love with Jeff. She reached the seventh floor and walked down the brightly lit hallway. The walls were clean and cream-colored with Victorian-style sconces lighting the way and antique gold mirrors in between each sconce.

Passing by the last gold-framed mirror, just before Jeff's door, she stopped and looked at her image reflecting back. She saw the glow of innocence delicately shining on her softened features. She thought, *Will I now lose the radiance on my face, or will I keep the rosy hue of my cheeks so from the outside, no one will be aware of my secret?*

She reached Jeff's door and lightly pushed the doorbell. With its ringing, it synchronized with her heart beating strongly in her chest. He opened the door and showed her the way in; she saw the table was set in colorful flowery tablecloth and napkins, with crystal wineglasses.

"I want you to enjoy the view of the ocean and the city. Come look through my picture window while I pour the wine, then we can settle down and eat. I have a special recipe I used for our dinner."

It was a beautiful sight as she admired the climbing roses that grew above the window from a flower box he had at the bottom of the window. The living room and dining area were neatly decorated in a country style of pink and lavender.

"I love the color scheme you chose for your apartment. It happens to be my favorite colors. I decorated my bedroom in lavender also. And the climbing roses, I don't think anyone would have thought of planting that particular type of flower in the house. By the way, you're a real chef. This fish is the best."

She slipped a note under his wineglass while he went into the kitchen to bring in the dessert and set it up in the living room. As he lifted the glass, the little paper was stuck to the bottom, which made them both laugh. Jeff peeled off the note and saw her words written so neatly: if I'm of the sea, then I'm your mermaid.

"Wow, I love your imagination. It helps you to write so lovely. Please keep writing to me. I love how you express your emotions, my little mermaid," he said, touching the tip of her nose, which made her face match the color of the wine.

"I have to confess that I did not tell anyone that I was meeting you tonight. I actually lied to my parents that I was going to the basketball game and out with my friends. Guess I'm feeling a little guilty now."

"Listen, I certainly understand this situation. Maybe someday in the future, like when you turn seventeen, I can meet them. This way, it would only be another year until you turn eighteen. Until then, it remains undisclosed. We are having an early dinner that coincides with the basketball game and the after-party, so no one will suspect."

As they put their wineglasses down, their eyes became connected and, with a deep silence, caught at each other's gaze. Jeff leaned to her, placing his hand on her neck as she reached for his arms and drew him closer. Their kiss lasted longer and became deeper until their passions took over with uncontrollable emotions. Their all-consuming passion for each other became lost in the waves of intense sexual ecstasy.

The beauty of sleep was like a sedative needed after their love-making; her head rested upon his chest, listening to his heart beating out a song to her. Her arms over his body and his legs wrapped around her, she traced the outline of his face with her finger and then realized how late it was, and with a jump, she woke Jeff.

"Jeff, it's so late. I have to get home. How will I explain the time?"

"It's not that late. Just an hour passed. I'll take you downstairs and get a cab. You will be home in no time, just say the game went into overtime. Call me before you go to bed. I'll be waiting. So don't worry. It will be fine."

She did not want to reveal her guilt to her parents, so with hiding her emotions, she quickly passed through their living room, singing and laughing about the fun she had with some friends. Then guilt-ridden, she turned to them and, with a demure look, began to explain her lateness.

"I apologize for my lateness, but I had so much fun. Even the after-party was late, and I couldn't just leave. I lost track of time," she pushed out the words, masking her nervousness.

Mother's humorous personality couldn't help but play along with her banter to Marina.

"It's okay, Marina. We had basketball games in the old days too, you know. We even got together after the games for ice cream. I'm not a cave girl, Marina. Get to sleep. Tell me about it in the morning."

In her room and under the covers, all she could do was think of all the wonderful moments that night with Jeff.

She quickly dialed his number and whispered into the receiver, "I'm home, and my parents didn't think much of the time. Actually, an hour overtime is really not that bad. My mom made a joke about it, so I feel much better about everything. I miss you already."

"I wish you could have stayed with me all night. I miss you so much. A night to remember," he whispered back to her as he leaned against his pillow.

"Oh yes, Jeff, it is a special night in my life to never forget. I'm so glad you were the one to give me this experience. My handsome man."

"Marina, my little mermaid, I thought that I could be a big boy and handle being apart from you, but that's not what's happening. I miss looking into those bright-blue eyes and the touch of your soft skin. I miss how you listen attentively to me. You make me feel important."

"I know, Jeff. I feel the same as you. It's your voice and your talk. I could listen to you forever, doesn't matter what you're saying. I miss you so much, but most of all, the way you touch me. You have become a silhouette in my mind when I'm not with you."

"Marina, beneath our talks lays our deep, connected love. Sleep now, mermaid."

As time went on in their relationship, they made their daily phone talks when they couldn't be together. They shared the love and passion for each other while waiting for their next arrangement to meet.

The next Saturday, Laurie stopped by to visit Marina. It had been a couple weeks that Marina did not call Laurie for their usual Saturday girl talks. Laurie felt rejected and questioned Marina where she had been.

"Hey, Marina, where in the world have you been? I miss you. It's been a while since we shared a Saturday morning like we used to. You don't call me as much, only sometimes after school. What's up with you? Why is it that we don't meet on Fridays anymore, and our Saturday-morning chats have stopped? I am really feeling disconnected and rejected."

"I am so sorry, Laurie. I didn't mean for this to happen. I have a confession to make. It's not you, and I think I pushed you away because I didn't want you to know the truth. Do you remember that handsome curator we met at the museum? Well, I've been dishonest with you and have been secretly meeting him. We have dinner together every Friday at his place and meet maybe a couple times a week. I am madly in love with him, and he feels the same way toward me. I believe we will get married as soon as I turn eighteen."

Laurie hung her mouth open, then with an uncomfortable swallow while taking a step back from her, she yelled at Marina, "Oh god, he is older than you. You should know better, and I'm sure by now you're having sex. If so, I hope you started birth control. If not, you have impaired judgment, and irreparable damage will be a result of this. You're only sixteen. How long do you think you can keep this a secret?"

With a flush that creeps across her cheeks and a sudden feeling of heaviness in her body, she lashed out at Laurie.

"We learned all about that stuff in sex-education class. I am sure to be careful because I follow the rhythm system. I know what I'm doing, and he understands to follow the same with me. We are both very careful, and you're so closed-minded," she defiantly answered as she tightly wrapped her arms around her knees in anger and hung her head.

Laurie had to stop biting her lip and calm down before speaking.

"I won't argue with you. This is just going to get out of hand. What's done is done. I won't reveal this to anyone because you are like my sister. We only have each other, no other cousins, and we always shared our secrets, so your secret remains with me. But please, let's go to the downtown clinic, and a doctor can examine you. Then he will start you on birth control. It's that easy. I know some girls who have been there and started the birth control pill. Please, Marina, let's go together. If you can't answer me now, let me know soon before something happens."

Laurie left with a knot in her stomach, so afraid that her cousin will get pregnant, but she knew she had to calm down and hope for the best and get on with her own studies.

CHAPTER 5

S pringtime finally arrived, filling Central Park with flowers blooming everywhere. With the scent of spring in the air, Marina couldn't help but feel in such high spirits. Jeff and Marina met early every Sunday morning at 7:00 AM in the Shakespeare Garden, sitting on the park bench and munching on bagels while she sipped her ice tea, and he drank his coffee. It was a secluded, intimate setting among the lush plants and flowers hidden between the Swedish Cottage and Belvedere Castle, and they pretended they were meeting as a duke and duchess.

It was their casual time to meet before he had to get back to the museum where he scheduled 9:00 AM morning tours that lasted throughout the day.

"We will meet up tonight again after I leave work at five p.m. I have a full schedule today, so dinnertime would be perfect, that's if it's not difficult for you to get away. I know Sundays are usually a family day."

"It's definitely a perfect time for me. I can get home now and spend the day with my parents. Fortunately, they are going out to dinner with friends around four o'clock, so it will be easy for me to meet up with you at your place."

With a quick kiss, they separated and went their own ways; he ran with a skip in the direction of the museum, and she on her way to the train to get home. As she sat in the train, she felt a little light-headed as before when they sat by the lake, but this felt a little different. When she got home, her parents left her a note that their plans changed, and they decided to spend the day at the antique conference and the evening with a group of friends for dinner. Marina was glad, since she wasn't feeling up to talking too much, so she took the opportunity to rest when a strange sensation of nausea filled her stomach, then she abruptly ran to her bathroom and began to vomit. She thought that bagel and cream cheese must have been bad.

The days that followed, she noticed her face became fuller, and her clothes didn't feel right around her waist. So she went to talk to her best friend and cousin, Laurie.

"I don't understand why I'm gaining so much weight, and I can't run in the gym like I used to. It's common for me to miss my periods every couple of months. Mom said it's a hormone thing, so I wouldn't think that I'm pregnant."

Laurie, filled with wisdom and much more mature than her cousin, already figured out the problem, and with a blank, motionless face, Laurie spewed out her feelings.

"I think you're pregnant! I'm taking you downtown to that clinic I told you about. Some of the girls from school go there for birth control. You will be tested and get the results right there. Let's go right now. We can skip the next class."

"Oh no! Not until I talk to Jeff. I'm going there at four o'clock when he leaves work for the day. I will talk to him about it then. It may not be what you're thinking. You're overexaggerating."

"Marina, what are you thinking? Is he going to be overjoyed about this? And you have to finish high school and go onto college. You and I made plans to get our degrees together."

"Stop the pressure, Laurie. I know him well, and I know what to do."

Both in anger, they went their different ways, Marina in high hopes that all would turn out great, Laurie having a feeling of doom for her cousin.

It was late afternoon when Marina arrived at Jeff's apartment. As they sat in Jeff's living room, she told him that she noticed weight gain. She explained that Laurie said she noticed a change in her face, that it seemed fuller.

"I have been feeling morning sickness, but thought it was just the bagel and cream cheese from the other day. Now I am frightened that Laurie could be right, but on the other thought, I always miss my periods."

Clutching his arms as his body stiffened, he narrowed his eyes toward her belly; slowly he reached and felt a small roundness. His mouth began to twitch as the color drained out of his face.

"You need to go with your cousin to that clinic today. The doctors there will examine you, and you will know for sure. You know you should have gone a year ago for the birth control. I can't believe you never did! I know we have been using the rhythm system, but you should have started the pill like all your friends did. If you're pregnant, it's probably only a few weeks, so it won't take long to abort. You will be able to just go home and rest. Your parents will never know, and you can continue with your studies."

Her face turned crimson as her expression hardened by his words.

She began shaking, clenching her fists, and with a quivering voice of despair, she said, "I thought we were in love and would get married when I turned eighteen. I didn't plan this on purpose, but it happened, and you are the father. You need to stand with me. You're the older one with maturity. why didn't you take care from the beginning? You've been having sex much longer than I have. So you want me to graduate? What an excuse for hiding the real reason—that this will only get in your way, right?"

He stood there with his arms crossed over his chest, shook his head, looked away, then released a breath, and with his eyes glaring at her in a different emotion, he said, "Marina, listen to me and be sensible. You have to understand that your graduation is only a year away. You have to graduate high school and go to college. This will only get in your way. Plus, I am really not ready to be a father now. I thought you were wise enough to go on the birth control pill. Not to mention that we are having such a good relationship. We do so many things together with freedom. Do you really think that a baby will make it better?"

Like dust coating her throat for a moment, she couldn't answer, then her body began quaking; dark emotions filled her mind as she felt trapped in her own body. She began screaming at him and repeating his words with clenched fists waving in his face.

"You're the older one. Why didn't you take care of this from the beginning? Why didn't we discuss this? So you say it will only get in my way. What you mean is it will get in your way! You have become toxic now in this relationship. I can't believe we are having this conversation. I already feel like you have abandoned me. I'll be eighteen this coming November. We can get married. I don't want to abort the baby."

"Marina, try to think rationally. What will your parents do about this? And what will they think of me? Our plans have perished. Your degree is gone."

Feeling faint and shamed, she ran out of the apartment and onto the elevator. Once she got to the sidewalk, she then gave a heave of vomit. She hailed a cab and got home and ran into her room. Her arms went limp as she tried to hold the phone, calling her only trusted friend and cousin.

"Laurie, please come here now while my parents are not home. I have to talk to you. I need help."

Her voice was raspy and in a low tone, almost becoming silent at the end of the call. When Laurie got there, Marina was hysterical. Laurie tried calming her down by helping her think this through.

"I guess you know you're pregnant, so now you have a big decision to make. First of all, I will go with you to tell your parents. You can't keep this a secret any longer because you are starting to show. Second of all, be ready if your parents tell you to have an abortion. You're a minor, so you have to do as they say."

"This is so much to think about, especially if my parents force me into an abortion. I would rather go away somewhere and have the baby. Or maybe they will let me stay here and finish school. They can care for the baby during the day. What do you think about that, Laurie? Tell me, is that a plan?"

Laurie just hung her head in disbelief, trying not to upset her anymore.

"Marina, I don't know if your parents or mine could care for a baby since they are so involved in traveling with their antique shows.

They own a business that takes a lot of their time. Please just let all this go until we talk to them."

"Oh, Laurie, I thought I knew him so well. I trusted him to give him my heart. I now know that he disguised himself. My innocence covered my eyes like a veil where I couldn't see what lies within his hideous heart."

She fell into Laurie's arms as they both shared in this terrible moment of the coming dreaded decision her parents will make and shared in the fear and tears of this doomed situation.

In defiance to Jeff's way of thinking about terminating her pregnancy, she thought he had no control over her body and what her decision would be. She definitely wanted to keep the baby in spite of his reaction. But she knew very well that the final decision would be her parents'.

The following two weeks were consumed with phone calls and packing. Marina's mind was clouded with thoughts of the life inside her and adopting out. She was glad that her parents didn't even think of abortion, or getting in touch with Jeff. There was no mercy for Jeff; all he was to her now was a villain. Her vision of him was of him rubbing his evil hands together like a devil that lurked in the shadows, and he took her, and she let him.

CHAPTER 6

A few days before their journey to Canada, Richard called his wife and daughter to the dining room table. As they walked in, they saw him sitting, holding his head and with an opened map. He held a red pencil in the other hand and seemed to be drawing on the map.

"Dear, what are you doing?" said Margaret with questionable eyes.

Marina, holding her belly, stared at her father then realized what he was doing.

"Dad, you figuring out how to get to The Fold, right?"

"Yes, sweetheart, it will be a very long ride, so I outlined all the stops for a stay over. It is actually fourteen and a half hours from here in New York City to Nova Scotia. That is a long ride, so I found about four different stopovers where we can rest overnight then have breakfast in the morning and start our trip again. If we leave here at 6:00 a.m., we will have reached at least Massachusetts in four hours."

"That sounds about right, dear. We can have a nice fish dinner, and Marina can rest."

Margaret turned to her daughter with loving eyes as he smoothed her hair with a mother's touch.

Richard then continued to explain their trip, outlining the route and all the stops, and then looked up at Marina with tears in his eyes.

"Sweetheart, this will all work out. We will enjoy our trip together, think of it as a vacation. You will be home before you know it, and begin a new life and finish your studies. We love you so very much."

Marina then went into her father's arms and just felt the comfort she needed at this stormy time in her life.

It was several uncomfortable hours in the car with Marina's parents as they drove to Canada. She was so thankful that Laurie suggested taking the ride with her to ease the tension. It had been a long couple of weeks for her parents to make arrangements for her to be sent to The Fold for unwed women.

"This is not what I anticipated. I am young and stupid. I should have thought with my brain, not my emotions," whispered Marina to Laurie.

"You can't just blame yourself. You both are responsible for this, but unfortunately, you will be the one to take on all of the emotional suffering. I am so sorry you have to go through this, but I am by your side, and your parents are being so helpful. This is the best for you and the baby. You will be home for the New Year and start fresh again. We will be back at school together and prepare for our graduation."

Laurie felt so deeply responsible for what happened between Marina and Jeff, wishing she hadn't pushed her to go out that night. Maybe then she wouldn't have met him. Because of their twin-like sister-cousin relationship, she secretly felt guilty and wished she could turn back time for her cousin but knew, in reality, they were both to blame.

Marina and her family have never toured Canada, so this trip not only a depressing time, but also a time to explore a little on their way.

"Girls, I thought since we are all going through such a depressing emotional time, I'd like to lighten it up a little by stopping at the artist alley. I found some brochures at the library and a map. There is also a French restaurant, which has a specialty made fish dinner." Richard tried to speak in a happy tone, knowing that his wife felt the stress of the situation.

"Yes, Richard, that's a good idea. You really studied up on Canada, didn't you? And I noticed you circled a bed and breakfast down the road from the fold."

Margaret gave a little melancholy sigh with a small thankful smile towards her husband but the tension had not lifted as yet.

The girls just sat in the back seat, feeling uncomfortable and waiting for their stop at the artist's alley so they could get up and stretch from the long ride.

By the time they were done with their tour and dinner, they were on their way to The Fold. There was a calm feeling for them all as they passed through farm areas with the white coral fencing keeping the horses safe. A bumpy dirt road led them to a turn, where a view of the sea with its crashing waves could be seen. Approaching the end of the road was their destination, with a sign "The Fold" just about a quarter mile to the entrance of the old plantation. At their arrival, the nuns who dedicated their lives to maintaining the facility greeted them. Marina noticed how impressive the outside of the old plantation-type house was, with its white pillars and green vines growing to the top and winding into the balcony where blooms of wisteria hung.

A young pregnant girl waddled her way to them with a large smile across her face, greeting them.

"Please be seated here and relax in our reception room while I let the director know you arrived."

They were seated on Victorian-type plush cushioned sofas while admiring the antique coffee tables. The tiffany lamps had unusual glass designs and gave a warm glow to the room. Consumed by the glamour of the antique-filled room brought her father a step back in time as they walked around, admiring and remarking of its value since that was his specialty.

"Dad, the ceilings are covered in ornate woodwork. Amazingly beautiful, don't you think?"

"Yes, Marina, you know I love that style, almost the same as what I had done in our living room."

As their conversations continued, her mother remained rigid and unable to relax with hidden fears for her daughter's future as she watched some of the young girls passing by.

Another young pregnant girl came out to greet them, pushing a glass tea cart filled with biscuits, cookies, and a white ceramic teapot.

"We have been waiting for your arrival and have prepared some refreshments for you. Please relax with some homemade cookies. Help yourself to some coffee or tea."

She walked over to Marina, smiling, and placed her hand on her shoulder in a comforting way as she began to describe the house.

"This was once an old plantation house, now it is a landmark here in Nova Scotia. We have ten acres fenced in by the white picket fence you see out there all around the property," she said, giving them a visual demonstration by spreading her arms wide in view of the scenery.

"Bedrooms have been added on this first floor, and upstairs six more have been renovated. We also have a reading room overlooking the Pacific Ocean, which is just a little walk down the south side. I go there when I need to be alone. You will enjoy the tranquility and the cool ocean breeze when sitting on the wraparound lanai. It will help you to think things through. But for now, just relax."

Then she hastily left the room.

Like the sound of a sergeant, a voice entered the room; it was the director dressed in a white uniform with a white hat upon her head.

"Allow me to introduce myself. I'm the director of the old establishment. My name is Ms. Stella, and I have been here for years. I can answer any of your questions, but first we need to take a short walk over to my private premises."

On their walk to the director's cottage, they all took a long look at the beautiful sight of the sea and all the surrounding land.

"Laurie, take a look at those magnificent oak trees. Must be over two hundred years old."

"Yes, Marina, such a beautiful, relaxing sight. The sea is magnificent with a nice scent blowing our way."

After the director's lengthy private conversation with Marina's parents, she called her to the desk and explained that papers had to be signed for her registration to live on the farm. Also, signature was required since her parents wanted her to have the baby adopted. Laurie held on to Marina's arm, knowing this was the most difficult time for her. Marina, feeling such a heavy weight in her arms, forced her hand firm to the pen and signed the paper; but in her heart, she was reluctant.

"We are done here. Let's take a walk back to the pavilion where the girls are waiting for us and wanting to spoil you with more of their homemade treats and tea."

They all rose to their feet, each one holding on to the other as they followed the director out of her cottage and into the main room of the pavilion.

"Cousin, I feel the strong arms of darkness holding me right now. I'm scared."

"Marina, it feels dark now, but remember, morning is promised us, and you will feel better once you settle in and get to know everyone."

When teatime was over, the director then called for one of the young girls to assist Marina to her room and asked her parents to also go to see where she would reside.

"I'm so pleased with the color scheme of white and lavender colors for the drapes and bedspread, even though the room is a little small, but it's just enough for you, Marina," Laurie said as she peeked into the closet and opened some dresser drawers.

"Yeah, I guess I can sleep here or sit on the overstuffed chair in the corner, and the footstool will help my future swollen ankles," Marina said with a giggle but felt a little paralyzed.

"Laurie, can you help me empty the suitcase?"

"Sure, Marina, I'll start hanging up you clothes in this very small closet," she said with a giggle and a softly deflating sigh.

When all was settled, clothes were put neatly away in the dresser; and once the clothes were hung up and arranged in the closet, it was time to say goodbye.

"Honey, we have to leave now and check into the bed and breakfast down the road. We have to wake up very early to leave in the morning. I feel you will be safe here, and you will finish your education and then come back home. I will miss you, and I love you so much."

Her mother just held her for a moment then quickly turned away, hiding her tears, and ran down the stairway.

Her father gave her strong hugs and tearful words of I love you; they huddled together tightly, not wanting to let go, then he followed his wife down the stairs.

Richard and Margaret sat in their car, waiting for Laurie, clinging to each other.

"I know this is a harrowing experience for us and everyone involved," Richard whispered to his wife.

"So painful, for Marina and for us. Our grandchild will haunt our hearts for the rest of our lives," Margaret cried as she held on to her husband's hands.

Laurie and Marina found great difficulty in separating.

"Marina, there are no words at this moment. You know how I feel. I'll be waiting for you to come home. In the meantime, keep the letters coming and make a phone call once in a while."

Then sorrowfully, Laurie departed, leaving Marina to sit on her bed, thinking about what her life has been. Then she sat crying and held her belly, soothing her child, hoping he or she didn't feel her emotional pain.

The Fold was interesting to Marina. It allowed her to take a few classes, especially creative writing class and earn some credits. The nuns were certified teachers and encouraged the girls, helping in their education. She became involved with their debate class and was made sure to go to church, which was on the premises. Besides the staff of nuns and a couple of nurses, a doctor joined the team. His living quarters were also nearby on the property. He had scheduled appointments for all the girls and was always assisted by the head nurse.

The hospital was only twenty minutes away, where Marina would give birth. Everything was arranged for her, like her education, for her giving birth, and for the dreaded adoption. Her deepest thoughts were that she felt like a victim; she could not believe that she was in this situation. *Everyone is making arrangements and decisions about my life, and no one knows the emptiness I feel in my heart.*

Even in this painful situation, she made sure to keep a diary of her life, living on this beautiful expanse of land. A bouquet of saltwater scent traveled into her room with the sea breeze. With the sound of seabirds calling her each day, she took her walk and settled down on one of the rocks. Some of the rocks had a likeness to large boulders projecting above the surface, where her imagination pictured a shipwreck from one of them. Watching the gentle movement of the waters swaying from side to side gave her peace, and she was able to write and compose her feelings into letters and notes. One of her poems she dedicated to Jeff:

> *It was easy with just one of your smiles. Then you marred my wholeness; I was baited with just a glance. I thought we would be two with a double heartbeat, but it was easy for you to separate. But there remains a double heartbeat here inside; it's mine and half of yours.*

Her time at The Fold moved quickly. It was December, and the cloudy sky gave a gentle snow, falling in rhythm with the slight breeze onto the open grounds. Marina sat in her room and watched the soft snowflakes through her bedroom window. Gently falling like a lullaby in the breeze, she wrote in her notebook for her child, and a feeling of peace flooded through her body:

> *What a beautiful sight, watching the snow falling; reminds me of a lullaby I could sing to my infant. In just a few more weeks into January, and I'll see my baby. Even for just a moment or a day, to hold and then say goodbye till I see her again.*

Holding her head in her hands and feeling a shiver run down her back, she decided to take her mind off all that she went through. So she went to check on everyone in the main room.

All the girls were downstairs in the large open foyer, decorating the big Christmas tree the doctor brought in fresh from one of the farms not too far away.

She took a few swaying short steps over to the balcony overlooking the downstairs main entrance room and wondered how they could all be so joyful knowing that they were also due to give up their babies.

"Hey, girls, I want to help but first would like to take a walk to the sea and feed the seabirds with the leftover breadcrumbs before it gets to dark."

"That's fine, Marina, but don't be too long. It gets dark early now. And we are having an early dinner tonight so we can have treats around the tree."

As she sat on her favorite rock, watching the birds and drift-wood, she kept thinking how nice it would be to never go back, but to go to her own home with her baby. *I want to run with the waves and see where it takes me. But reality tells me, just go back and wait for January when I will see my baby.*

As she sat, she could feel her baby moving, turning, and push-ing very hard.

"I love you," she whispered to her full-grown belly and began writing a poem to her unborn baby:

> *I closed my heart after you were born, drowning in a sea of infinite isolation, but my never-ending notes to you will remain folded away because you were taken away; my heart will not be filled until we meet again.*

It was early twilight when she realized she stayed longer than wanting to, so she decided to leave when a current of wind mixed with snow started blowing against her, making it harder to walk. Struggling against it, she started feeling weak; within minutes, a sharp pain shot across her belly, causing her to fall forward. The pain was intense, and she realized her water broke, so she tried to lift herself, but the pain became fierce. She screamed above the ocean's evening roar, hoping they would hear her. She wasn't that far from the side windows of the house; she could see a warm glow from the front porch light.

With the house being isolated at the end of a road and fearing the savage wind blowing off the water would drown out her cries, she tried screaming louder above the deafening roar.

Back at the pavilion, in all of the festivities, one of the girls noticed that Marina had been missing too long.

"It's been a while that Marina has been gone. I'll run upstairs to see if she slipped passed us."

The director became concerned with the panicked sound of the girls calling out her name. The doctor and director ran out onto the front porch, but the snow began falling into small snowdrifts, blocking their vision. They decided to run onto the grounds; as they started running down the south side of the land, they heard Marina's cries. With a struggle lifting her, they helped her to the house, and the doctor realized she was about to give birth.

"We will never make it to the hospital, so let's prepare her in our small medical unit."

The doctor and nurses scrambled to prepare Marina, knowing that within minutes, this baby will be born. Marina felt a painful flush along her face and neck that travelled down her back. Her belly tightened and as she screamed with her whole body, but she did not feel her mouth move. She lay still for a minute, sweat dripping from her face, thinking this pain was ongoing agony. One of the nuns helped by pushing against her back to keep her up; she went forward, and the pains came faster. Marina then began grasping and digging deeply in someone's arms. With each painful push, she gasped for breath, then with a piercing scream, called out Jeff's name, cursing him and damming him to hell. Those in the room felt her emotional hurt but continued to coach her through the birthing process. After about an hour of pushing, her screams tore through like a great shard of glass, as she could feel the hot stretching of her inner body; and with a final shrill and push, her baby was born. The nurse ran out of the doors in great excitement and made the announcement about the newborn.

"It's a red-haired baby girl!"

Marina could hear the cheering and applause, which made her feel proud through the tears.

"I can't believe how the human body can withstand such trauma as birth," she expressed while trying to take control of her breaths.

"Oh yes, Marina, you have just experienced part of being a woman—birthing."

The nurse replied as she swaddled the little girl and handed her to Marina.

Marina was so happy there didn't seem to be any resemblance to Jeff. Her one tiny red curl on the top of her head and little blue eyes just melted her heart. She held her close and tight and took each breath of this little one. As she pressed her nose against her newborn, taking in long deep sniffs of the sweet smell of her infant, she thought this scent would never leave her.

As she placed her baby closer to her neck, she whispered in her ear. "Daughter, as I keep your sweet infant smell locked in my memory, you also will have a remembrance of our heartbeats. I will not be there when you take your first steps or for your birthdays. But I will remember this day because I gave birth to you, and we will be tied to each other in a mysterious way. You may not know now, but someday we will meet face to face, and we will recognize each other. I will never leave you, and you will always be with me. I will always be with you, even when you leave here."

Just then, the nurse came in and said she would like to take a picture. Marina gestured yes, and with the old Polaroid camera, the picture was taken and left by her side.

Soon after the director walked into her room like an army officer in a snowstorm.

"In about a day or so, a couple will arrive at my private premises and sign for the baby. I will explain why you want to name the baby Seton, but remember, they will most likely have a new birth certificate drawn up for everyone's protection."

That night, Marina was allowed to sleep in the same room with the baby by her side in the bassinet. She couldn't sleep; she was in awe of this beautiful being.

As she gently caressed her, she whispered to her, "I love the feel of your tiny fingers curled around my pinky. I must enjoy you for just this little while. Since you were almost born at the sea and on a farm, I'll name you Seton—that means Farm by the Sea, but our secret is that backward, Seton means Notes! Someday you will figure that out and question it and find that I have stored up notes for you to read when we meet again. I am sure you have this generational gift of composing, someday I will read your notes also."

The next morning came to soon; the nurse came into her room, helping her to prepare for the infant's departure. Even with the assistance of the nurse, the walk down the staircase seemed to last forever while holding her infant tightly in her arms. Her legs began to feel heavy, hard to lift, like a dead man walking, but she kept walking down the hallway into the foyer. She sat down with frozen arms, increasing her grip on the baby, her heart rate rising, giving her a dry mouth and a sudden impulse to run. The nurse's echoing words broke her thoughts.

"Marina, please let go. I must take the baby to the director's house. Someone will take you back to your room now."

Like in a dream woken by her piercing tone, still feeling almost unconscious and unresponsive, mechanically she raised her arms slowly, almost smoothly, upward, releasing the baby into the nurse's arms.

Gripping the arm of the chair, she weakly pushed herself up and was assisted back to her room. She clasped her hand on the railing as she walked up the steps, feeling the numbness and heaviness in her now-empty arms. But in her mind, she cursed Jeff for this terrible transition and for the pain in her heart that felt like broken glass chips cutting her insides.

She sat in her overstuffed chair with her hands holding the once-swollen belly, wishing this never happened. She heard a car starting up and listened as tires rolled down the graveled driveway, wanting to take a peek out the window but too weak to get up and knowing that the sound was taking her daughter away.

In a while, the director walked into her room to give her some counseling, hoping to help her to become ready for her own future.

"What you are feeling right now is a great loss and a normal physical reaction. Your body is changing as your hormones will be changing also over this month. We will help you to regain your strength, and then you must resume your studies."

As she left, she placed a cup of tea on the nightstand with the picture the nurse took of her holding her baby. The rest of the girls all went to their rooms, for they also felt her pain and knew that their time approached. Marina just sat and stared out the window at the sea. She faintly heard the seagulls in the distance, and the breeze brought in the smell of the sea, but this time, it changed. There wasn't an ocean aroma, but the smell of dead algae. As dead as the winter snow and as silent as the night, she felt alone again.

She watched the delicate swirly sparkles the hoarfrost left on her bedroom window. Her eyes traced the patterns of frosted lace on the window, reminding her of the baby's future beautiful white lace christening gown for her baptism day.

I wish I had not listened to my parents or anyone else about having strangers adopt my child. I should have run away to another part of the world. This baby was life inside me, now she has another new life. Maybe the beating of my heart will follow her, and she will remember my heartbeat and remember me someday, she thought.

As she held the picture of her daughter all wrapped in pink, placing the picture against her chest onto her heart, she kept it there inside her shirt.

Darkness covered the sky again; there were no stars that night, just the crashing waves against the boulders that once led her to writing, now just a clattering noise. Like the sound of violent crashing, breaking falling pieces of destruction, her thoughts tangled in a maze of confusion.

CHAPTER 7

I t was still December, and Laurie was home, thinking of her cousin Marina and remembering how she was by her side when Marina made the announcement of her pregnancy and would stand with her through all the families' battle about it. Laurie and Marina were born in the same month of November. Although Marina was born on the twentieth, Laurie was born on the seventeenth. They would often kid about Laurie being older than Marina.

Laurie respected that her parents were very secretive and private people, where she learned to also be confidential with her friends' problems, especially her cousin's. She heard stories of good deeds her parents did for people in need from the antique functions she attended with them. They never spoke of their past lives, only some sharing about their parents and how they both were an only child. She often wondered why Marina was the only one she knew in their small family that had the glossy red hair.

With her hands on her hips and in a strong stance Laurie questioned her mother, "Mom, Marina's hair is a beautiful red, and I'm the boring brown. I want highlights in my hair."

"All right now, Laurie. There is nothing wrong with brunette. It is not boring brown, and sure, why not get some highlights? It doesn't matter to me anyway. You are my beautiful daughter."

Her mother started winking and flipping her hair in a fun way and walking circles around Laurie.

"But I still don't understand why her hair is different from mine. Actually, no one in our family has that color. After all, we are cousins, and there should be some kind of resemblance. And I'm sure someone in our ancestry had her color, don't you think so?"

Laurie questioned her mother with and inquisitive stare and an inquiring tone in her voice.

"Yes, Laurie, someone in our lineage had red hair, but since I never knew anyone beyond my parents, I wouldn't know who! I never knew my grandparents from either side. Your father and I don't even have cousins. I'm so thankful I had you, and at least I have a niece."

She turned to Laurie with her round face, which was filled with rosy cheeks as her whole face turned red. She felt her daughter was a little intrusive, so she started to change the subject.

"By the way, my little missy, I'm glad you're accepting the college offer from Hunter. I'm sure Marina will do the same. So you two can travel together through college as you have through high school."

"Yes, Mom, just six more months, and we will graduate from high school and onto college. I can't believe how quickly time is going for us."

This following day, Laurie thought maybe she read her mother wrong, so with her inquisitive nature, she began investigating into her parents' private office. As she walked into their walk-in closet, she never noticed before that there was an extended part of the closet that resembled a hallway. So she began walking deeper inside, pushing away cobwebs and afraid of meeting up with a spider's home. With dust flying, she finally came to an old file cabinet.

She gingerly pulled out the top drawer, only to find old bills and order forms for antiques. Then she pulled out the second bottom drawer, where there were so much more papers and envelopes with old dates and stuffed so sloppily. Her fingers felt their way, passed more old documents until she reached to the back of all the envelopes; there was one that stood out among the rest. She saw a yellow legal-size envelope with some old-brown age spots on it. It lay nestled alone all the way in the back. She pulled it up and out and noticed it had someone's handwriting written on the top labeled "Notes for C."

Being a curious girl, she opened it and found one long white envelope addressed to Cinderella with so many little notes inside. The second white long-size envelope, also addressed to Cinderella, contained one written letter. Wondering who Cinderella was, she carefully opened the smaller one and began to read a couple of little notes. Each note was handwritten with memories from someone named Julie.

One note was written, *The sea brought you to me.* Another was written, *I loved you the moment I heard the news.*

My secret cry flows to you, and we will meet again.

I can still see you when I walk to the sea.

Today would have been your first birthday; you must be walking by now.

I can still feel your heartbeat. Can you hear mine?

Laurie proceeded to open the second white envelope; there was a date scribbled on top of the page, November 20, 1950. As she read the letter, she could feel heavy emotions written on the page. Tears covered her face as she felt so much love coming from this Julie to Cinderella. After about an hour, she decided to close it up and leave so no one would know she was in there.

Laurie thought, *These notes and letters were written so long ago and hidden here. I feel such a broken heart from this person, and I know there is more to this. I will get to the truth, but they are on their way back, so I'll get back to this another time.*

Throughout the course of the day and night, the words on the notes and the letter continued to stay with her. She felt emotional pain from this person who wrote all these notes to Cinderella, and she kept thinking about who Julie and Cinderella were and why this was kept a secret.

The journey of time went on, as the two girls graduated together and began their internships with prestigious publishing newspapers, where they faced a new life and new complicated situations.

"I'm really glad that we live in close proximity to each other, after going to high school together then college and onto graduation. Who would have thought we would be traveling to a job together!" Marina expressed with a twinkle in her eye as she spoke to Laurie.

"Yes, cous, I am enjoying my training for paralegal at the Legal Aid Society, thanks to all my studies in legal research at Hunter. With my great hopes, I will be a lawyer. I feel my life is so exciting now."

"So true, Laurie. I feel so free since I started my internship at The Post, but I still carry a secret pain forever in my heart. I'll never stop thinking of her. I think of her every day and remember how she felt in my arms, so tiny. But that part of my life is long gone now and thanks to the creative writing class that has led me to study journalism, where I can continue writing and exploring. Both our lives have changed for the very best. Come on now. Let's squeeze our pinkies for forever friends, forever cousin."

Marina Cynthia enjoyed her early morning wake up since she started her internship at The New York Post as the editorial assistant in the administrative office. Observing and assisting the freelance writers gave her great possibilities in writing.

This is a great opportunity for me to learn more about writing articles and editing, working under specific editors. I can become respected as a writer, and I will fulfill my dreams as a journalist, she thought.

She never really paid attention to her looks, just a quick brush of the hair and up in a messy bun and out the door, sipping her coffee. This one particular morning, as she brushed her hair in the usual way, she took a strong look in her mirror and became lost in its reflection. Noticing the few freckles running across her cheekbones and her large blue eyes, she encountered a memory of her past life and a broken soul. Her hair changed from bright red to a darker color. She realized she wasn't a young girl anymore and wouldn't want to go back to that time in her life ever again. Leaning closer to the mirror, a myriad of emotions overcame her as she felt she looked directly at her daughter.

What would my life be like now if I had not given her away? Where is she living and what is she doing at this exact moment? Is there a resemblance that we both inherited by ancestors we never met? Do we share these bright-blue eyes and red hair? Does she have my smile, or is this just fragments of windblown thoughts? Marina wondered.

Remembering she had an old photograph to keep when she gave birth to Seton, she frantically went through her closet and found the old box she kept up high on the top shelf. There on the bottom of the box under letters she had written to Seton to help her grief was the faded Polaroid picture of her holding Seton. She sat, holding the picture as her tears fell, almost fading the appearance of the photo.

It has been six years now, and my Seton would not know me if she saw me. Being so busy with straightening out my life, I often wondered if she looked like me. Does she have my personality? I can still smell her scent after all this time, she thought.

Her reminiscing only brought her to the bad memories of Jeff, the father of her child who never made an appearance or contacted her parents. Word went around that he was not working at the museum any longer. She thought he made his great escape somewhere, never to return. Had he done this before and run away, leaving someone else abandoned with a baby? She was deceived, as Eve was with the craftiness of the serpent, which was Jeff. Examining her skin with still no trace of wrinkles, she thought time has been good to her, but time has buried memories as deep as the ocean; and like the hourglass, the passage of time moved slowly.

A few weeks later, Laurie thought to follow her instinct about Marina. Laurie was calm in nature but carried an investigative trait, so studying to be a lawyer was a perfect match to her personality. This natural tendency brought her to look into the meanings of names like Cinderella.

She went to the New York Public Library and found books upon books of definitions. When she came across the name Cynthia, its definition was from Cinderella. She looked up Marina and found it means, "From the sea." She put it all together and realized that Marina Cynthia was "Of the Sea Cinderella." Holding her breath for a moment in disbelief, she realized this could be her cousin.

Laurie thought, *This is a very well-kept secret, which needs to be unearthed, with questions answered about her biological parents and if this is really true. I do not think I am exaggerating this discovery, for I believe this is my cousin. Marina is Cinderella! Then who is Julie? I have to get some help with this. Something is awry, twisted!*

The following Saturday morning Laurie and her mother decided to have breakfast together, while her father went to help his brother, Marina's father, at the antique store.

"Mom, why is Marina's middle name Cynthia? What does it stand for? Was she named after someone special?"

Laurie's mother almost choked on her coffee.

"What do you mean? We call her Marina, but Cindy for short. Why the sudden interest in her name?"

Laurie noticed her mother's face turning red and knew there was more to this story and needed to press her more.

"I don't have a middle name, and she does. I'm just Laurie."

"Well, Just Laurie, the French meaning to your name is really pronounced Lorcan, meaning fierce. I knew you were fierce when I gave birth to you, so your name is fitting."

They both laughed uncontrollably.

"Well, Mom, my fierceness will make me a great lawyer, don't you think?"

"Goodness, yes, Laurie, and I'm proud of you and your great accomplishment."

Laurie's mother tried to mask the truth in her eyes, spoke in confidence and control while she clasped and unclasped her hands.

A couple of weeks later Laurie and Marina's parents went to a conference, and Laurie asked her father for permission to invite just a few colleagues over for hors d' oeuvres and wine.

"Of course, we trust you because you have grown so maturely in your new career at Legal Aid Society. We are so proud of you! You and Marina enjoy your new friends, but make sure there is always order in our house. I don't want to come home to a mess!" her father answered with a wink of his eye at her in a comedic joke.

The date was set for that Saturday night, about ten from Laurie's classes and ten from Marina's classes. Their excitement grew with the anticipation that together they would be hosting their first college party.

CHAPTER 8

With each ring of the doorbell, another person or couple entered the apartment. Finally, the count of people was more than twenty friends attending this social gathering. Marina checked the freezer for more food for the crowd and was happy to find enough to warm up. As she brought more snacks on a silver serving tray, she noticed one man on the other side of the living room leaning against the fireplace. Their eyes connected through the throng of guests, and they gave each other a sunny smile. Even though the crowd thickened, Marina made respectful conversation with everyone she just met and the ones she already knew. But there was one man she took sight of as she observed his gestures while speaking to his friends.

He's really cute but overfriendly, talking to everyone on sight, yet a gentleness and politeness flows from him. I could drown in his deep brown eyes, and so round with dark, long lashes. I really shouldn't be thinking like this. I'm so busy with work I don't need another man to ruin my life, Marina thought.

As she gave him the once-over, he suddenly turned, facing her; and as she examined his chiseled features, she noticed he walked her way. She became frozen in her spot.

As he approached her, he couldn't help but notice the blue in her eyes and her long lashes and tiny freckles running across her nose.

She must be a natural beauty; I don't see makeup on her. And those eyes are such a deep blue. Her freckles are red color, which makes her so adorable to look at. I never saw her at the school, but I have to meet her now. While in his deep thoughts, he found himself magically walking closer toward her.

Then clearing his tightened throat, he said, "I couldn't help but notice your wavy red hair from across the room, so I thought I should introduce myself to you. My name is Michael and yours?" He made a gesture with his hand rolling downward and laughing.

Her supple cheeks blushed as she batted her eyelashes, and with a coy voice, she answered, "I'm Marina. Glad to meet you. Laurie is my cousin, and we are hosting this party together. We both invited at least ten apiece, but it looks like a lot more have invited themselves."

She answered by lifting her shoulders slightly in wonder to him of the increased number of guests from her list.

"Well, I must say I love your name. It's very musical, sends a breeze my way when I say it. I know Laurie from the Legal Aid Society, but I never saw you in any of my other classes."

"We both graduated together, but I was in the journalism class and was hired at The Post."

Both laughing and feeling the heat in their faces, they continued their conversations for hours. Finally, by 3:00 AM the party shifted to goodbyes and good night.

Laurie noticed the two of them in deep conversation and made her way toward them to ask for help.

"Excuse me, but we are all tired, and as you can see, everyone has left, or maybe you want to be a part of the cleanup crew," she jokingly said with a gesture of her thumb.

"I never realized the time. This guy is a real talker." Marina giggled as she glanced up at him.

"People in the room? I saw no one and didn't realize anyone was in the room with us. She kept me occupied and triggered my senses."

Michael pointed his finger toward her then shook it at her and laughed. They all joined in a burst of laughter, and they started walking to the door.

"I was thinking we have a lot more to talk about, so let's get together for dinner. what do you think?" His eyes widened as to what her answer would be.

"I would love to have dinner with you. You could explain in detail your law experiences, and I could write a story about you." Her eyes flickered, and she gave him a crinkled nose.

They exchanged phone numbers and set the date for the coming Saturday.

"I'll call you Friday, Marina, then you can give me your address again, and I'll let you know what time I'll pick you up."

"I'll be waiting." Not only her cheeks, but also her whole face, turned rosy red.

After they cleaned up, she walked home and started remembering what she already went through. The past life experience was so much for her emotionally. Hoping she was not jumping into something that will only leave her hurt again, she began thinking about his eyes and the gentleness that he showed. As Marina cuddled under her warm lilac comforter, she pushed away all thoughts except Michael's face. His mild-mannered nature was so natural, giving her a relaxing feeling for the first time in a long time. Rethinking and replaying their conversation from the evening, she decided to think of him as Michael like Michael the Archangel.

As she slowly slipped into a dream state of fantasy and her surroundings slowly drifted away, she whispered, "Maybe he's my archangel."

The following Friday night they met at The Garden Room. It was exactly how Michael described the little cozy, hidden-away Italian restaurant. There were just enough tables scattered in the dim candlelit room, where the walls were covered in deep, rich red bricks from ceiling to floor. Tiny arched recessed coves holding votive candles, catching little lights in a hue of silver and blues shining against the walls, gave her a feeling of being in the grotto. The gleam of marble tiles displayed an Italian design that caught her eyes with each step she placed on its curved stone under her feet. Flowery vines draped the walls, climbing to the ceiling as the antique-green Italian stone planter urns filled with colorful flowers were placed in every direction, filling the room with a perfume scent in the air.

At the end of the tiny restaurant was a table for two adjacent to a huge wall fireplace with ember glows placing shadows against the wall. It was a perfect romantic night where they were able to talk and share about their future dreams. Their deep connection started as night went into early morning. They decided that this was their own private place to meet each week. They prolonged their goodbyes with an emotional hug, which lasted a little longer than expected.

Michael whispered in her ear, "I'll call you tomorrow."

As they separated with arms stretching to their fingertips and a momentary turn away, like wheels quickly turning, they swung around to get a last glimpse of each other until their shadows vanished out of sight.

Sunday morning was quiet for Marina, as her parents were not back from their weekend conference, so she called Laurie to come over and sit to talk.

"Wasn't it great, meeting so many new people from our classes? We have great friends with a goal in life. We are headed in the right direction. I'm so happy we had the party. I also noticed you and Michael made a connection."

"Oh yes, Laurie, we did, and I feel we were meant for each other."

"Well, don't rush into this, but tell me about Friday night with him. What is he really like, and does he have charm? Does he eat fast?" Laurie asked, brushing her palms together in excitement.

"Oh, Laurie, he took me to this little, hidden Italian Restaurant where we sat for hours talking. I felt so comfortable with him. We talked about school, our graduation, and our families. I told him how you are more of a sister to me than a cousin. He loved that and wished his family were bigger. He has one sister, very young, about six years old. He was in high school at Valley Forge Military School when she was born. Once he graduated, he went straight to your law school department at Hunter," Marina spoke with dreamy eyes, flashing her lashes at Laurie.

"Well, Marina, I never saw him at school possibly because he's a year younger than us, so he wouldn't have been in any of my classes, but so strange that we work in the same law firm. And now that I know he's twenty-two, and you're twenty-three, you're robbing the cradle!"

Now both rolled on the bed in convulsive, childlike laughter.

The week dragged on for Marina, waiting for Michael to call her for another date. Thinking maybe he was not interested anymore, she decided to give him a call.

"Hey, Michael, it's Marina. I thought I'd say hello. It's been a while since we talked and had such a great dinner. How are you?"

"Oh, Marina, I had you on my mind all week. I'm working on an important case, which keeps me busy till late evening. Please forgive me. Tomorrow is Friday. Let's meet at our favorite restaurant. This way we can catch up on our weeklong workweek."

"Definitely yes. The Garden—it is my favorite restaurant now. I was hoping you would say that. We do have a lot to catch up. Can't wait."

They met that Friday, and the waiter remembered them from the previous date; with a wink, he brought them to the same table.

"This case I'm working on is classified, so I can't go into detail. I have been in work by 7 AM and don't leave until around 9 PM. I have been exhausted, and with all the research I have been doing it has given me so much more knowledge about different cases. I'm sorry for not calling you. I hope you understand how I became so involved with this case." His tone of excitement turned to a loving gaze behind his black-rimmed glasses and into her eyes.

"I am intrigued with your profession and could never judge you for all the work that you do in this corporate world. You are passionate and determined in your work for the courtroom. And you never know, I might need a lawyer someday."

With a sly smile, she glanced up as her eyes widened to show how impressed she was with him.

She told him all that she learned and experienced at The Post, as he sat with alertness, his eyes fixed on her every word. During their dinner, he was able to share with her what it was like in military school.

"Don't get me wrong now when I say I do appreciate what my parents did for me by sending me away to military school. It was the best education ever, and it's what brought me to study law.

But I missed the fragrance of the country life where I was raised in Tennessee."

"How I would love that, since I never lived outside of New York City. It would be nice to get away from the hustle and bustle of the city to the quietness of the country. Maybe if I lived there, my life would have been extremely different." As she spoke, she focused on an empty space in the air between them, remembering the life she did live while a teenager and the emotional pain that remained.

"Growing up on lots of property with sweet pine trees and especially the magnificent blossoms of the magnolia tree, with its lemony-sweet scent was a wholesome way to grow, then being sent the opposite way of life in military school was a shock to my system."

"Well, maybe if I was a country girl, we would have met sooner, at one of the chicken fries that you mentioned that you went to on Friday nights."

With fingertips touching over the table, he said with an arched eyebrow, "Well, maybe when we are finished with all our internships and establish our professions, we can go visit."

The evening repeated as before, and they knew they shared a deep affection and passion for each other. They knew it happened when their eyes first met.

She saw his demure character with warmth rushing through his soft brown eyes, and his smile ever so genuinely sweet. She thought, *He is tall and handsome and a well-bred fellow. I need him in my life.*

She had to tell him what she felt, so she softly spoke to him, "I think of you the first moment when I wake up, with my first sip of coffee."

As he gazed upon the softness of her face, he couldn't help but tell her, "I fall asleep with you on my mind. Sometimes I can't even sleep."

She spoke softly, almost a whisper as she focused on his lips, waiting for another answer.

They walked holding hands in a freestyle motion as the sounds of the city made music for them.

The Garden Room became their regular weekly meeting after work each Friday 7:00 PM. The waiter knew exactly without a question, and with a nod of his head, they followed him to their spot by the fireplace. They became such regulars the waiter expected them each week and always had their table ready for them in their private corner of the room. They became more interested in each other and found so many similarities. Both loving the mountains and hiking winding paths in the Adirondack Mountains, they both agreed it was time to spend weekends escaping to the mountains.

This one particular weekend, as they were hiked, they stopped and sat on a small log overlooking a waterfall. They felt vapors of water rising, and in the mist, he snatched her hand and squeezed it, then they found their lips and arms entwined; she felt his gentle yet strong touch caressing her breasts. As he buried his face in her neck, she clutched his body, fusing together in their moment of love. The waterfall and leaves became distant sounds as he drowned in his pleasures of her body. Clutching her waist, he held her tight against his chest, where their heartbeats linked to each other's, and they became weak in the intimacy of body and mind.

A few weeks later, Marina knew it was time to tell Laurie of the good news about her relationship with Michael.

"It finally happened, Laurie. I met the man I will marry. He is coming for dinner next week. I have to tell my parents all about it, but I had to tell you first. Once the time is set, you and your parents can come for dessert. I want him to know the little family that I have. From our first date, we knew we were serious with each other, and now we both know it is time to meet our families."

Marina walked fast in circles with excitement, and her voice quivered with joy.

"Well, of course, we will be there. After all, he will be my brother-in-law. I'm so happy for you. This is the best news in such a long time. We will have so much planning to do." Laurie leaned forward from her sitting position on the bed and with eyes glowing cries with joy about the good news.

But she nervously began biting down on her lip as she brought up a dreadful question, "Did you discuss what you went through with Jeff? I mean, the relationship and the baby, what was his reaction?"

"I told him about my disastrous relationship with Jeff, but that was it. I can't talk about the baby—it hurts my mind and heart."

"But he needs to know what you went through and help you. If he really loves you, it won't matter. Maybe someday he can help you to find her."

"*No,* it's over! I am already living in the shadows of my sin. I don't need to bring up my past. When I think about it, I feel like my insides are going to explode. It was the worst time of my life, and I buried it. Now I am living the best time of my life. I do not need any interruptions. I deserve happiness, and now I have it."

"You're being sibylline, so mysterious. You can't start a relationship like this, Marina. Think what would happen in the future if he finds out. What a shock it would be."

Laurie realized the conversation was going nowhere and didn't want to upset Marina at such a happy moment. She backed down on the conversation, apologized, but left upset. After already reading notes about Cinderella and finding out some truths, she felt it was only fair for him to know so he can help her to find out hidden secrets and bring them to light. But this wasn't the time, she thought.

Months rolled on as they anticipated so much for their future together, so again they went to their favorite Friday dinner at The Garden. As Marina lifted her fork, she noticed a piece of paper under her plate. She slowly removed it and cautiously opened it. Sunset was written on it.

"Why?" she asked.

"Your hair," he answered. "Red, and your red freckles that sweep across your cheeks."

"Oh," she replied, "you're a poet also."

They laughed, but deep inside her heart, as much as she loved this romance, it only brought back memories of Jeff.

What would have led him to do this, I feel like I'm reliving something regrettable. But he's different from Jeff. He shows signs of compassion. I was the one to start this with Jeff, this is very different, and it's reversed. I shouldn't compare, she thought.

Each Friday his notes expressed his deepest feelings for her, and with a blush, she accepted but also wanted to express her own inner feelings. On the following dinner date, she put a note under his dish before he arrived.

"Oh, are we taking turns now? You're a copycat."

Laughing, he removed the note and opened it.

He read, "Butterflies," and asked, "Why an insect?"

"You added colors and the sweetness of nectar to my life, and I feel butterflies in my stomach when I think of you."

The notes continued with each Friday-night dinner. Notes upon notes, month upon month Marina collected each treasured note, saving them in an old shoebox to be read over and over again. As she labeled the box, Notes, she felt a chill through her body as she remembered the word notes when reversed meant Seton.

CHAPTER 9

This one particular Sunday morning her parents, Margaret and Richard, were home, not attending their usual antique business, so she was sure to surprise them with breakfast. They sat together, talking about her weekend.

"Mom, he is so genuine, so deep. We have been dating for a few months. I didn't tell you because I think he and I both wanted to make sure before we tell our families. We are truly in love, and soon our parents will meet."

Her parents were so surprised, and with astonishment, they jumped up and began hugging Marina.

"Oh, sweetie, I am so happy that you found someone to love. This is wonderful. Our family will grow now."

Richard gently squeezed her shoulders, holding back tears of joy.

"Tell us more. What is he like? What is his family like?"

Margaret hardly got the words out fast enough.

"He was raised in Tennessee, and his parents still live there with his little sister. He wants to make plans for me to visit them very soon. So we have to set a date for him to have dinner with us."

"Oh, Marina, this is thrilling. He wants to meet us. This means he is very serious," her mother cried out in joy as she held her chest.

"Yes, this is great. I am finally getting a son-in-law!" Father's words radiated outward through the room proudly as a smile stretched across his face while lovingly patting Marina's head.

"And grandchildren. Yes, our family will grow." Mother held her arms, as if rocking a baby, and laughed.

"Well, you both look like you just won a million dollars," Marina replied with a wide-open grin she could not cover.

They all, in a silly manner, giggled at all the thoughts they shared for this happy moment. Their laughter began with giggles and turned to waves of hilarity.

Then Marina's father sat down with a very serious expression and reminded her of the turbulent time she once had.

"Sweetheart, I guess you talked with Michael about what happened when you were only sixteen."

"Of course, I did. I told him how young I was and was fooled by Jeff. That he left for somewhere, and no one knows where. I did not speak about the baby. It is too early in the relationship. Just the thought of what I did brings so much emotional pain. I cannot talk about it. It is something that will forever hide in my heart. She has a perfect life now. She will never know what happened, and no one else will. This conversation is over and done as of now."

Her father tried again to talk about the situation, trying to be in control, and talked with a soothing voice, wanting her to understand the dangers of covering a lie.

"Marina, that part of your life was part of ours, and we also have regrets of what happened to you and our grandchild. But we especially know and have learned that this is a situation that should not be concealed. He loves you, this is evident, so he will understand. Please do not be ashamed. We will stand with you and explain how we all felt at that time. What if the child tried to find you someday? Think of these things."

"Yes, Marina, our lives are filled with choices—some good some bad. You can change all that with a good choice we find from a sense of love and loyalty for others. Think of sharing this with Michael and someday searching together for her," her mother said and leaned closer across the table to her with hands covering Marina's, waiting for a response.

With an intense feeling of rage and agitation, her jaw muscles tightened, and she blatantly gave her feelings, "It is a buried issue. A secret sin buried with the dead part of my heart. I have a new life now, and my heart has been restored. I want to live it with him, so stop this ceaseless questioning."

Giving them a dramatic rejection of their advice and threatening them that if they tried to reveal this, she will disown them, she slammed her bedroom door behind her and jumped onto her bed in tears.

Bombarding me with questions about this secret that I have enshrined in my heart and mind. They stormed me with memories and besiege me. I blocked those memories of emotions and grief only for them to unlock it and to haunt me again, she thought.

Her parents returned to their own room with a feeling of failure for also concealing the same situation about her. They often wondered why she never questioned that her face did not mirror theirs. They feared her reaction to this recent argument will be the same when they share the secrecy of her being adopted. They felt the adoption was something that needed to be hidden and not revealed at any time in the past or future. There were times they hoped when she came of age, they would share the truth of her identity; but as time went on, they became consumed with her life and parenting, so they became fearful of that time of truth.

As the days passed, the tension between the three grew, and Marina made sure to avoid her parents whenever she could. But the sadness drained each of them, and although silent, it was engraved on their faces.

"Richard, I sometimes feel like ice was poured down my back when she walks into the room."

"I know, dear. Let's just keep our opinions and our tears inside, hidden like under leaves so we can keep peace between each other."

Days moved on, and Richard and Margaret kept their feelings hidden so as not to have any arguments with Marina. There was a kind of tiredness that overcame their bodies and spirit, as if needing a good night's sleep but never finding it. The wearing down of emotions only gave them a sense of silence that grew wider between them.

Marina sat in her room this one night, trying to concentrate on her work when she began to realize, her emotions of rage, anger, and love for her parents struggled in her mind.

"Why am I punishing them for my past actions? They lived through my pain with me, and now I do not show any thankfulness. Their love is eternal, and I disrespected them. I have to change that now," she said to herself.

She walked into the living room where her parents sat and read the newspaper. She sat down next to her father. He looked up at her, and in that moment, he saw a flash of darkness in her eyes. He took her in his arms and held her.

"Marina, nothing can separate a parents' love for their child. What happened and what was said last week is now over. My love for you is stronger than keeping a disagreement. You are right. The issue is laid to rest."

She stayed in his arms for a while as he rocked her calm and steady, as if she were his little girl again.

The following week was the dinner date set for Michael to come meet the family.

Marina's mother ran around that Saturday, arranging the table with her fine china and soup in a special soup tureen.

"This is a great celebration. I feel like dancing," Margaret sang around the kitchen as Marina watched and laughed with tears of happiness in her eyes

"Yes, Mother, and this fish has a remarkable aroma. I hope I can cook like you."

"Well, ladies, I just finished my help with the dinner table with our fine-china dishes. I hope you think it's presentable for Michael."

"Oh, Dad, thank you so much for helping. You will love Michael. He is just as helpful as you. You two will definitely bond."

Just then the doorbell rang, and Marina went running to bring Michael in.

After their introductions, they sat in the living room, getting to know each other while sipping on a cherry cordial.

"Well, Michael, I understand you will be a fabulous lawyer." Richard's eyes set straight into Michael's and raised an eyebrow.

"I really hope so. The corporate world is a difficult one, but I really hope to service those in need with pro bono for the public good while I also continue my legal work."

"You sound like your fervent determination and strength will help you in the courtroom," Richard replied with satisfaction.

Margaret then announced that dinner was ready, and all sat in the dining room.

"Mom, the candles are beautiful, making our dinner so romantic," Marina giggled while her eyes met Michael's, and they both grinned and winked at each other.

"I must say, this fish dinner is as tasty as The Garden restaurant. You will have to meet the chef there," Michael said, smiling as he sparked Margaret's interest, complimenting her dinner.

When dinner was over, all helped to clear the table, while Richard invited Michael to join him in the living room for an after-dinner drink.

"Richard, I'm glad we get to have a minute alone. There is something I'd like to talk with you about."

Richard tilted his head in a glimpse of understanding what was about to be asked.

"Go ahead, young man. I think I understand what you want to talk about."

"Richard, I truly love your daughter. I never felt like this before, so I want to ask you if you would agree with me to propose to your daughter."

Richard rose from his seat and extended his hand, clasping Michael's into his with a strong hold.

"Michael, I agree, and I know that you are both adults, and you are anchored in love and respect. I give you my blessing."

"Thank you, Richard. I will go this week for the ring. Can I call you and let you know when I will surprise her?"

"Yes please. Actually, come here when it's done, and we will have a drink of celebration together. I am sure she will want us to see the ring."

Just as their conversation ended, Marina walked into the room with a tray of pastries and coffee.

"Hey, you two, you have a serious look on your faces. What's the conversation about?"

"Darling daughter, just man talk, nothing to worry about unless you want to talk about the football trade?"

You could hear the joyful laughter like a waterfall flowing through the room. It was at that time they became warmly connected. Enjoying this precious moment, the four of them became the fabric of a family.

A few weeks later, Michael mentioned his parents were inquisitive about her. Since they only know her name, they would like to meet her. Marina agreed to set a date to travel to Tennessee with Michael. One night, as they sat on the beach at dusk, enjoying the pink-and-purple sky, he turned to her and saw the glow in her eyes reflecting the sunset.

"I feel so intertwined, as if our souls are stitched together. Nothing can interrupt our lives. We were meant for each other till death do us part," Michael whispered in her ear while holding her in his arms.

"I to feel so connected with you. When I am not with you, I feel you inside my soul. I want nothing to interrupt our happiness and our relationship," she replied back to him.

"Oh, Marina, how could anything change our world of love and bliss?"

This one particular dinner night at their usual corner of the restaurant, she looked for the note that was always placed under her dinner plate. As she looked up, she noticed his face was a little red, as if he was embarrassed, but there was a little smirk at the corner of his mouth. With a wave of his hand, their waiter, Angelo, came by with a bottle of champagne and placed it down. She noticed a note under the champagne bottle. Puzzled, she took it out and opened it, and it read the words she longed to hear: Marina, would you marry me?

Her eyes flooded with tears as she looked up, and he stood over her, holding a diamond ring in his hand. She jumped up into his arms as a definite yes. The entire restaurant with its customers began shouting congratulations and waved their napkins up in the air.

Angelo stood by, crying as if it were his children. It was a great night of celebration in their favorite place.

Walking home, the moonlight cast a soft white glow for their path, revealing their shadows on the sidewalk. An outline of their figures united into one as they linked arm in arm as if afraid to lose one another. With warmth running through his body, he quietly and gently said as he touched her cheek softly, "The moon is shedding its luminous glow all around us, casting our shadows on the sidewalk. Look how our shadows have merged just as I said we are one."

As she lifted her eyes to him, caressing his face and reaching for his lips, she placed a soft kiss.

"How could we unfasten what has already been sewn together?"

CHAPTER 10

Within two weeks, their air flight was scheduled, and they began their trip to Nashville, Tennessee. Once they landed, a comfortable car was ready for leasing, and they began the drive to his hometown.

"Just about one more hour, and we will be in the town of Goodletsville where I grew up. You will love our house with four bedrooms, and wait until you see the backyard, if you want to call it that. It is more like the land of a plantation. My family has been waiting a long time to meet you. They are so excited about this."

"I feel so nervous meeting your family. My hands are actually shaking and so sweaty I think the ring will fall off."

They both laughed as Michael reassured her that they already felt like they knew her, and his little sister was so excited.

"I can't wait to meet your little sister. She must be so cute. We will surprise her and ask her to be in the wedding party. And there is so much to talk about with your parents I don't know where to start."

"My little sister is a princess. She always wears frilly dresses, and then again after school, she's in jeans and climbing trees. But wearing a little bride's dress as a flower girl, I can't wait to see her expression about this. And absolutely no worries about meeting my parents. They are cool and calm just like most people in the South. They love to talk and have the gift of hospitality. Wait till you see how comfortable they make you feel."

They drove through hills and roads lined with trees. She understood why he grew up such a well-mannered man. Everything seemed so calm and serene, and she smelled the Tennessee air with its rich fragrance of untouched land with flowers blooming everywhere. *What a change in lifestyle*, she thought from living in the city all these years and never venturing out into the country. As they approached his home, she saw wisteria growing on the two front trees. *How beautiful*, she thought as they passed by, driving on a very long, graveled driveway.

"As you can see, our house is about one thousand feet from the front road up to the front of the house. Most houses are built far back from the road for privacy. Wait until you see all the acres of land with groves of trees we have. It's a beautiful sight."

As Michael pulled the car up to the house, the front door quickly opened, and out jumped a little bouncy six-year-old girl. She ran straight to Michael and jumped right into his arms, squeezing him and smothering him with kisses. He laughed hysterically as he held her and said how much he missed her.

Marina watched this loving moment between brother and little sister then noticed her tiny body and her bright red hair tied up in a ponytail.

Red hair, bright-red hair like mine used to be, she thought.

"Marina, come closer. Meet my little sis. Cordelia, this is Marina."

Marina knelt down on one knee with hands held out and so to get a closer look. The child ran right to her and locked her arms around Marina's neck; at that moment she felt the little heartbeat against her chest. In that silent time of tenderness, Marina felt a flush and stirred with strong emotions. With this affect, she released the child and quickly jumped to her feet, hoping no one noticed. Not understanding why she felt so strange, bewildered she quickly whirled around, glad that everyone still talked and laughed with Michael. As she turned, his parents ran to her, greeting her with such excitement and open arms.

"Marina, this is truly a wonderful moment. Let's all go inside and settle down."

Michael's mother brought Marina up to her room where she would be staying for the visit. They made themselves comfortable on the bed, talking about the travel from New York to Tennessee.

"Let me see your hand, sweetie. What a beautiful oval-shaped diamond my son gave to you. It reminds me of my engagement day with my husband. Such an exciting, eventful day to remember."

With a look of admiration and love, she held Marina's hand in hers, giving her such a warm welcome to the family.

Marina thought, *What a courteous woman she is and such a gentle spirit. I can see where Michael inherited her genes.* Marina patted her hand in return.

She stroked Marina's hair, smoothing it lovingly, as if she were her child, and spoke in a soft tone, almost as if it were Michael, "I really hope to get to know you very well as I welcome you to my home and into my family. We do need to expand our family, and I believe you will fit in perfectly. After all, if Michael picked you, I trust he picked the best."

Marina knew that by her facial appearance and charming personality, she would make a pleasant mother-in-law. So flattered she embraced her with joyful tears and felt a strong connection.

Marina's eyes flickered with excitement.

"Lenora, I feel so comfortable now, and I know my parents will feel the same when they meet you. They send their regards and an open invitation to come visit in New York and stay with us. We have plenty of room, and they can't wait to show you my father's antique store. Then they plan on taking you on a New York City tour. So please check your calendar and set a date. I will call you when I get back home so they can talk to you by phone, which is what they have been wanting to do."

"This sounds like a magnificent plan for us all. It will be our family trip to New York, but most importantly, becoming a family with your parents. Well, dear, now I'll go downstairs and finish up dinner for us. Come down as soon as you are ready so we can all discuss this together."

As she quickly left the bedroom, a slight breeze kept the door scarcely open, giving Michael's little sister a chance to peek into the room. Marina noticed the little girl's ocean-blue eyes shining through the opening with her little fingers holding on to the side of the door.

"Don't be shy. Come in here. Come on now. Let's talk"

Cordelia jumped and rolled on the bed with loud giggles as if being tickled. Marina noticed the roundness of her big blue eyes as she playfully touched the tip of her nose, giving it a pinch. With a closer look, she noticed the tiny freckles running over her nose and onto her cheeks.

She is adorable; oddly enough, we have the same eyes and freckles, she thought.

"You're such a tiny thing. Do you eat enough?" Marina said as she pulled on her ponytail.

"I eat everything on my plate even though I don't like peas. Dad said if I don't eat them, I can't go outside."

"You know, I don't like peas either, never did. They are yucky, but same as you, my parents made me eat peas!"

"I wrote that down in my composition book where I keep all my thoughts. I call it the complaint page. That's in the back of the book. The front has happy thoughts."

Strange that she has the gift of writing; it must come from her brother, since he's the lawyer, she thought.

"That's a great idea. I don't have a composition book, but I do have a writer's log where I keep my thoughts so I can eventually put it into either poetry or some kind of writing. Do you think you can share yours with me someday?"

"Sure thing. I will someday. But you will have to read yours to me also." Cordelia covered her mouth to whisper almost in an utterance and with giggles.

"Shh, it's our secret, little one. No one will know we write poems." Marina mimicked Cordelia, and they laughed together jokingly.

Marina lay next to her as they faced each other, sharing their secret about their personal writings and laughing about their words swarming in their mind. In their close presence was a familiar scent, like a warm breeze of innocence that rose from Cordelia. Marina felt a connection at a deeper level, as if bonded souls. Her breathing slowed as a dull memory captured her thought then quickly brushed it off as just a disturbing sensation.

"Marina, I love your hair. It's so soft, just like mine," Cordelia squealed as she tossed Marina's hair with her little fingers.

Cordelia's words broke into Marina's thoughts.

"Oh, Cordelia, you're amazing. You're so bright for only six years old. You must be the best student in your class."

"Oh yes, I get all A's in my report card. Every time I bring home a good report, my parents reward me. They take me to my favorite ice cream parlor in the center of Nashville." Cordelia laughed and licked her lips, pretending she had ice cream.

"You know, you are important in my life, especially since my brother has always been so far away. Now I'll have you around more often, like a sister."

The child also felt something unusual toward Marina, a kind of hidden emotion, and did not know how to express it. They continued a little girl conversation, asking each other questions about where they lived, school, their friends, and family life.

This child is really bright and talks like an adult. I am enjoying her so much. Strange that we like the same things—she likes to put her thoughts on paper same as me. If her hair was a little darker red, we could be sisters, Marina thought.

There was a dinner call from downstairs, and Cordelia was the first to make a dash down the staircase, with Marina trying to keep up with her. They were all seated in a large dining room. The table was a beautiful, hand-carved oak table with two matching oak hutches, which held Lenora's fine chinaware. The wall was covered with an old-fashioned print wallpaper of soft gold and pastel green, giving such warmth. With Mother at one end and Father at the other of the table, they all held hands, bowed their heads while Father said the dinner prayer.

Father's strong voice asked all the questions and kept the conversations going.

"Tell us what is it like growing up in New York City. It's definitely different from living in the country."

"It wasn't so bad growing up as an only child, especially since my best friend and cousin, Laurie, lives right around the corner from me. We grew up as sisters. We went to the same school all the way through college. Even though we now have different professions, we still we take the same train together two times a week," Marina explained to Joseph as she motioned to Lenora with a smile and nod about the good dinner.

"Well, I basically grew up in Pennsylvania for military school, but my early years were here in the south of Tennessee. As I always told my parents, I'm glad I had the experience of both lives. Now, who would have thought I would be in New York City interning as a lawyer? I'm glad I did get there though, or I wouldn't have met Marina," Michael said with glinting eyes and spread his hands toward Marina.

"Here in Tennessee, we felt Michael wasn't getting the early education we wanted for him. Although the colleges are excellent, we believed that military school would help him be a stronger person. Of course, he was the only child at the time. Until we had our surprise package." Mother crinkled the corners of her eyes to Cordelia.

"Yes, what a surprise. While I'm away, a little bundle was born. I just wish I was home for her birth. But anyway, I was happy that it was the school holiday, so I was able to come home to see my new baby sister," Michael replied as he reached over to Cordelia and pulled her hair.

Dinnertime lasted a long time, with all the eating and long, enjoyable conversations. When dinner was over, everyone helped to clean up and put everything away, then Cordelia grabbed Marina's arm, tugging her to the back door.

"Come with me now outside. I want to show you my favorite tree I climb in."

"Yes, let's go. I want to see all the acreage Michael told me about and your special tree."

Covering her eyes from the setting sun, Marina was amazed at the size of the backyard; it was far from usual, and it traveled for miles.

"Why are there so many birds in your backyard?" asked Marina as they flew overhead, casting their shadows on the grass.

"They are our blackbirds. We feed them the crumbs every night. They like it here. Sometimes they get real close to me if I'm sitting on the steps. They know me well. I even gave them names." Cordelia continued to throw the bread crumbs onto the ground, watching the blackbirds dive downward.

They walked along a stream that seemed to float along the side of the property until they came to a pond where ducks and swans gracefully moved in ebb and flow, making ripples in the pond. There was a little wooden shed on the side of the pond and a ramp way leading up to an open door.

"What is the purpose of the shed with the ramp? Does anyone walk up there?" Marina asked, puzzled.

"Oh, my dad said that sometimes the ducks and swans need shelter, especially if it's raining. So he built that for them. He said you must always take care of the animals."

Cordelia still giggled at Marina, thinking she asked funny questions.

"Cordelia, I can't believe how far we just walked to get to the pond. how far are you taking me?"

Marina felt like she had walked a good half hour from the house already and was getting tired. Cordelia gave a little giggle.

"We have so much property that everything is spread out. that's why the pond is so far from the back of the house. But we are still safe cause my dad had our property fenced in."

They started walking up an elevated part of the property. once standing over it, Cordelia yelled loudly, calling out and pointing to the far left of the property. It was the biggest willow tree Marina ever saw, so extremely tall and full.

"Wow, even though I have lived in the city and have seen the willow trees in central park, I have never seen this size before. It is amazing!"

Cordelia ran ahead with such speed and shimmied her way half-way up the tree before Marina could catch up to her.

"You seem to know you're way very well on this property, young lady, and how did you learn how to climb up a tree as fast as a fox?"

"Mom said I've been doing this since I was a baby. Come on up."

So Marina clumsily tried to put her feet into each niche that she saw Cordelia use. Fortunately, the first branch was just high enough for Marina to reach without too much exhaustion.

With Marina sitting close to the trunk of the tree for her own safety, Cordelia sat next to her and showed her how much farther the property went. There were so many trees, trees of every type sending out so many different fragrances.

"With so many trees, how do you know what they all are? I only know of the maple tree since that is basically what is planted near where I live." Marina stared with eyes wide at the sight of the grove of trees.

Cordelia called out in her little voice, naming each tree, and with her finger pointing to each one.

"Maple tree, oak tree, and birch tree, and one of my favorites is the apple trees. It's my mom's favorite because she always makes fresh apple pie for us. But this big willow tree is actually my true favorite."

As they sat on the thick, sturdy branch with feet dangling, Cordelia pointed out some wild horses running freely way back at the end of the property.

"This is a beautiful sight, watching beautiful creatures run wild and free. I can understand why you come here, Cordelia."

The grass is greener, and the scent of Tennessee is strong and pleasant. Maybe this is where I am supposed to be, Marina thought.

As they sat on the tree, Marina studied Cordelia's profile and thought how beautiful and smart she was. *I really love her. Why has she touched my heart so deeply?* she thought

"Where are your friends, Cordelia? It seems like no one lives close by."

"I have some friends, and I am in a dance class all year, but over the summer, I joined a swim club, so I am very busy, but I like to come here and sit and read my books. Father said it was fine. He can see me from the back porch."

"Well now, he must have very good vision. This is quite far from the house. I would have to use binoculars."

"No need to worry. This is my favorite spot, and I come here every day after school, and sometimes I do my homework sitting under this tree. During summer early in the morning, after I feed the birds, I walk here after breakfast and read and write a little bit," she said as she picked at the bark and tried to throw it as far as she could.

"My goodness, what could you be writing at six years old? You must have some imagination," Marina said with a giggle.

"Just whatever I see, like the opossums living in the top of the tree. When I come here at night, I can see their dark, tiny black eyes looking down at me, and they are pretty friendly. They don't bite, you know, and they come down and eat the oranges I bring with me."

Marina noticed the sun was really setting, and after checking her wristwatch, she realized they had been gone over an hour.

"We should probably get back home now. It's getting late. I don't want your parents to think I kidnapped you."

"Oh yeah, I forgot about the time, and it's dessert time now. Mother is probably ready to serve now. We better hurry."

With a quick jump to the ground and a quick dash, Cordelia started running across the field, while Marina still tried to get down from the amazing willow tree.

"Here come the girls. Please wash up. It's dessert time," Lenora called out to everyone in the kitchen as she watched the girls running in the back door.

"I'm sorry we took so long, but Cordelia really knows a lot about her property, and it was a lot of walking that I am not used to." Marina laughed and showed Lenora she was out of breath.

"Okay, Cordelia. May I join you in the hand washing."

Before she could even finish her sentence, Cordelia already had the chair pulled up to the sink and began washing her hands.

"It seems she enjoys jumping all the time. She took quite a jump off that tree. I could barely keep up with her." She smiled at Lenora while she also scrubbed her hands with Cordelia.

With a wink of her eye, Lenora joined in the laugh. Just then Michael walked in the room, leaning against the doorway; his eyes sparkled, and he felt a warm feeling at the sight of his little sister and future wife enjoying their time together.

All were seated again in the dining room, which was set for dessert with coffee and tea. In the middle of the dining-room table was a very large homemade apple pie.

"See, I told you mom loves to bake apple pie. she does every week, sometimes more than that," Michael said, taking a spoonful of pie as Cordelia wiggled and giggle in her seat.

The taste of fresh apple pie with apples picked right from the backyard tree was indescribable for Marina.

"You will have to teach me this recipe. I have never enjoyed apple pie so much before. Back home, it's either from the deli as my father comes home, or sometimes he takes a little longer route to get to a really good bakery."

"Wait until you have the next piece with our homemade vanilla ice cream and topped with homemade whipped cream. My wife is the best with making all this from scratch recipes. This is where I gain all my weight." Joseph held his coffee cup up, as if making a toast to his wife.

Marina thought, *he is quite big and very tall. His voice is so strong and deep. But he is a merry person and easy to get along with. I will enjoy having him as my father-in-law.*

With all the excitement and conversations, she found herself speaking so fast with such excitement her words came out all twisted, and everyone thought she was so funny and laughed.

"Marina has an announcement for all of us to hear, especially for a little person sitting at this table."

With that, Marina turned to Cordelia with a wide smile; leaning toward her with elbows on the table, she propped her chin in her hands.

"I am in need of a small person to fit into a little gown for a flower girl. But she is so small I can't find her," Marina laughed as she looked under the table, as if searching, then looked up and stared at Cordelia.

"How would you like to be in our wedding party as the flower girl?"

Cordelia jumped up from the table and bounced on her toes and started dancing with happy tears, screaming yes in a high-pitched voice. Then she ran to Marina, and with a hug and a kiss, she bounced her way to Michael and squeezed his neck.

"What color will I be wearing, and what does the dress look like, will I wear pumps, and can I wear makeup?"

The questions went on continuously until Dad had to calm her down. They began discussing the colors of the wedding party and how they have to visit a few small wedding halls. After that is set, Michael's parents and sister can come for their visit and they will take Cordelia to a wedding dress center to pick out her flower-girl gown and shoes.

"As soon as everything is arranged, we will fly out to New York and spend time with your parents and, of course, your cousin Laurie and her parents. I'd like to talk with them about the arrangements and get to know each other now that we are family."

Lenora wiped her eyes with happy tears while holding Marina's hand.

After the dessert clean-up time, Michael grabbed Marina's hand.

"Let's go out back and take a walk in the moonlight."

The familiar path she took earlier with Cordelia changed with each step on the soft grass she took with Michael. He took her to the same willow tree, where they lay down in the lush grass and enjoyed the blanket of stars above them as the moon gave a lightly lit sky.

"There is such beauty in the sky," Marina said as she lay in his arms, watching the twinkling stars.

With firm eye contact centered on hers, he whispered, "The only beauty here is you."

In the quiet, star-studded night, they surrendered to each other as he took her in his strong arms. As night fell with a deep dark blue haze, an orchestra of subtle tones of nature mixed with their whispers of rhythmic utterances to each other, were heard only by the great willow.

A week passed, and they knew their vacation time had come to an end, so packing became the next detail on their list. As Marina filled her suitcase, little Cordelia ran into her room and jumped on the bed. Marina could only laugh and lay down next to her, both nose-to-nose laughing and making jokes.

"I feel like I already met you, and 'cause now you're my sister, please come back soon. I love you."

"I love you so much, little one. I will come back, but don't forget, you are coming to visit me in the big city very soon."

This time Cordelia didn't jump off the bed; she slowly walked to the top of the stairs then turned her face around to look back at Marina. She gazed into Marina's eyes for a moment then walked down the staircase to wait for Marina and Michael to load up the car.

Marina felt unsettled by this, and being alone with her thoughts as she finished packing, she felt this strange feeling in the pit of her stomach and started shaking. She thought, *This felt like I held her before. Oh, but this is ridiculous. This must be my blood sugar dropping again.*

They all walked humbly to the car together, saying their goodbyes with lots of hugs, kisses, and tears. At a slow pace, they drove down the driveway with continuous waves. Marina and Cordelia's eyes could not disengage until finally, the car was out of sight. Lenora noticed a perplexed expression on her Cordelia.

Being concerned, she questioned her, "Sweetie, what's wrong? Are you sad that they are leaving? You don't seem like yourself. You seem troubled."

"Mom, I don't know. I feel like she's my sister, but I feel like I already knew her," Cordelia spoke quietly, withdrawn, as she watched the car like a speck in the distance.

Throughout the ride to the airport and onto the plane, Marina could not shake off this feeling of déjà vu. After landing in New York, they decided to go back to Michael's apartment for a while. She sat with a hardened expression as sadness on her face.

"Seems like wine is my comfort drink. after our road trip and air flight, I need to gradually wind down." Marina sat, holding her glass of wine with a clouded look on her face.

Michael's face went blank as he sat down, crossing his arms over his knees, shaking his head.

"What's wrong? This sounds like a complaint, and you're not yourself. I never saw you like this before. Listen, if you're just nervous over the whole family meeting and wedding planning, it's all going to work out. You connected with my family, especially Cordelia. You were meant to meet them and are meant to be a part of my family."

"You're right, Michael. it's just the jitters. It's been a busy week, and now we both have to get ready for work."

"Yup, fun is over, back to work for both of us. You go home and get some rest. I'm going to sleep now, and I feel exhausted also."

When she arrived home, her parents were already asleep; she was glad she didn't feel like talking about her vacation yet. She sat on her bed and relived her time with, Cordelia. The feelings of familiarity remained with her strongly about the little girl; she could not let go of the strong deep connection she felt and the strange unique scent that seemed to flow around her, and it captured Marina's soul.

CHAPTER 11

The following Saturday morning Marina's parents left to attend another antique seminar with Laurie's parents. The girls planned on spending the weekend together. Just like old times, their laughter rang through the rooms as they sat on Marina's bed, talking about their memories and now living in the future that they planned.

"Laurie, I can't explain this strong connection I feel with Cordelia. It is so strange that she is somewhat like me. I mean, even though she's just a little girl, she likes to write same as I. She has a little notebook that she keeps all her writings in. Only difference is, she is a country girl, and I'm the city girl. At first, I thought of it as a foundation for family and a sense of belonging to them all. But this emotional connection I have with Cordelia is almost a reflection of me in so many different ways, I feel some kind of soul tie. Here, take a look at our family picture her mother had printed for me from their pharmacy."

Laurie looked and noticed that the little girl had a likeness to when Marina was young. Absorbed by this conversation, Laurie knew that it was time for Marina to learn of all the information she stored up.

"Okay, Marina, I wasn't going to tell you, but I think it's time. I found hidden documents in my parents' room. I really need to show you so let's get there now, since no one is around, and figure this all out together."

Puzzled yet curious, Marina followed, having Cordelia on her mind, thinking it has to do with Michael. It felt like a long dark narrow corridor as their hands felt, along the unfinished part of the closet walls. Pushing aside cobwebs, they finally found the end of the closet. Laurie reached up and turned on the one light bulb that was over the file cabinet.

"I have been going through this for months then decided to keep it a secret, but after a year of this, I feel now is the time. I wasn't going to show you this. I am afraid that it will cause a war in our family. We have never kept secrets between us, so I believe you should be aware of what I found."

She carefully took out a very large yellow envelope, which was folded in half and stuck far into the back of the cabinet. She also had another one hidden that was a white envelope, which Laurie made sure to keep it in a safe place, containing information she secretly investigated and some truths. The tiny room was dark with only one overhead bulb giving just enough light to read.

Marina carefully opened the yellow envelope, which contained many papers that fell out, addressed to Cinderella. Then a long white envelope also addressed to Cinderella. Marina opened the white one, and it was a handwritten letter expressing her love for her baby daughter and with regret that she must turn her over legally to adoptive parents. The letter went on to explain her love for an older man in a small town in Canada. As she read, she felt herself tightly gripping the paper as her face became contorted with shock and pain. She sat slumped over the letter and notes that fell on the floor. With her eyes widened in fear, and as if the room was far away, feeling faintness, she gazed up toward Laurie.

"Laurie, please tell me, who do you think Cinderella is? It's me, isn't it?"

"Marina, I have already investigated all this. I didn't tell you because I had to make sure. Please don't be angry with me that I went ahead without you in this matter. You have to read these papers also."

As if tremors took over her hands, Laurie gave Marina another white envelope. There were two papers clipped together.

The first one was an actual legally stamped birth certificate:

Child Name: Cinderella Cynthia Gagnon.
Born: 12:00 AM. *Date*: November 20, 1950.
Father: unknown.
Mother: Julie Gagnon.
Place of Birth: Nova Scotia, Canada.

The second one was another birth certificate:

Name: Marina Cynthia Martin.
Born 12 AM. *Date*: November 20, 1950.
Father: Richard John Martin.
Mother: Margaret Roseanne Martin.
Place of Birth: New York City

Laurie then went on to explained she took the liberty to investigate and went to the local State Department of Health and showed both birth certificates.

"I was questioned why I needed this information, so I showed them my credentials as a lawyer and certified to investigate. After they accepted my investigation, they then explained it is official that this child's birth certificate was a new birth record created by the registrar's office. Marina, you already know that this is an official procedure for adoptive parents to maintain confidentiality."

A thunderbolt of awakening overcame Marina; as the blood left her face, she became white as stone. Laurie quickly shook her out of this sudden, disturbing news. She brought her back to her bedroom to rest.

"I feel like I am in a dream, as if I am on the outside looking in. This really isn't me. Why is this happening? Why did I find this out so late? Why didn't my parents tell me this sooner?"

Traumatized by this information, she gathered up all the papers and notes and went to sit down in the living room to talk through this with Laurie.

"I feel distressed right now. So we are really not blood related, you're not my real cousin. They are not my biological parents. I have no family!"

"Stop! Marina I am and always will be your cousin and sister. You can't remove all the memories we have stored in our lives. Yes, this is a great big lie, but let's try to understand why your parents hid this. I believe it was fear of losing you. And I don't want to lose you now. Listen, when they all get home, we will present all this information to them. You are in shock, and they will also when they find out what we found. Then they will accuse me for the investigation, not understanding that this is my personality, that's why I am so good at my job."

They went back to Marina's apartment, and Laurie stayed over, not wanting to leave Marina in the state of mind she was in. Laurie also wanted to question her own parents for keeping this secret in their private files. For this reason she wanted to face them all with Marina.

The next morning murmur of voices could be heard coming from the kitchen into Marina's bedroom. An aromatic scent woke the girls to follow into the kitchen for a morning cup of coffee. As they walked into the kitchen, all the parents casually sat and sipped their coffee; when they glanced up, they saw an unusual tense look on their faces.

Laurie's mom invited them to sit and enjoy breakfast with them.

"Good morning, girls. Sit with us for breakfast. We brought special croissants."

"I'm glad you are all here together because I have something to say," Marina said, still standing with the envelope in her hand.

The room was filled with an anxious feeling as all eyes became wide and ceased blinking for a moment. Marina held on to the documents as she sat down with lips mashed tightly together and eyes narrowed down on the papers. She read allowed the differences of the two birth certificates then held them up high for all to view.

"I now have misplaced trust by you who I thought were my parents. This wound has compromised the feeling of love and security, especially the feeling of belonging as a family. You both, you all lied to me. How embarrassed I feel about being the only one who didn't know!"

Was it the coffee burning or the smell of ashes from a volcanic eruption that made her parents feel as if they would crumble to the floor? Her father sat with his mouth gape open and became frozen. Her mother felt as though her own breath was trapped inside her throat.

As her mother shuddered at the tone of Marina's voice, she then lowered her head and spoke in a trembling voice, "This is not the way we intended for you to find out. We kept putting it off, afraid that you would leave us. When the doctors told us, I could not have children, we filed for adoption, and with their advice and help, we were sent to Canada. Just one look at you in your pink blanket, and we fell in love and promised we would give you the best life anyone could have. Believe me, Marina, so many times we privately discussed this, trying to figure when to tell you. But watching you grow and loving you so much, we just could not tell you."

Marina's parents were determined to explain the value of her existence for them, but feeling betrayed and once again abandoned, Marina's words stung in argument with her family as she refused to accept their explanations.

"Do you mean you adopted me at The Fold, where I gave up Seton? Is that why you knew where to take me? That's why you already had a connection in just two weeks!" Letting out a harsh breath, she slammed the documents onto the table.

Worn out and exhausted from this argument, so low in spirit as they continued to labor in their claim of rights in adopting her, she continued to believe that the evidence she held in her hands was proof of their lies to her.

She halted in midsentence. "Any further argument I have with you will now die on my lips."

Her eyes bored into theirs as she slowly turned away from them, raising her hand as if holding back a strong wind.

Laurie and her parents quickly stormed out of the apartment in tears. Marina, in a rage, stormed into her room and locked the door. A sharp pain slithered between her temples, fogging her thoughts between loving her parents and hating them. Holding the documents against her chest brought back the memory of her also holding her infant daughter and having to surrender her rights as a mother. This Julie had to give up her own possession, the gift of a child. Marina's mind filled with questions storming like a hurricane with thoughts of Julie, her biological mother, and this family, which was the only family she knew.

Sitting back on her bed, holding on to a big, overstuffed pillow, she began to rethink everything that she just went through. Her heart ached that she hurt her parents with words she could not take back. She thought of the time she came home to tell them she was pregnant and the situation with Jeff. How they cried with her and stood by her. The decision to give up their grandchild was just as difficult for them as it was for her to forsake her child. She squeezed her eyes shut as the thought of when she threatened to disown them if they revealed her past; thinking twice about that now, it would be the same as when she had to surrender her baby.

A realization came slow but clear to Marina as she thought how her biological mother, Julie, also having to relinquish her rights to her infant, gave Marina a new look at this recurring nightmare. She decided to approach them and settle this, knowing that their love for each other was strong enough for them to face the difficulties of this turbulent situation.

As she entered the living room, she saw them in tears, hunched over and holding on to each other in despair. Feeling their heartbreak, she then understood, and even though she still felt numb from the shock of her adoption news, she walked over to them, feeling the love she always knew, wrapped her arms around them, and cried with them.

Margaret's eyes grew dull as she gave a soft look upward to Marina.

"Dear Marina, pain is pain. Only our details are different."

Rubbing her tearful eyes, she sat close and cuddled her mother's hand in hers.

"I know, Mom. You will always be my parents. You loved me so much I would have never thought I was adopted. You raised me to be an intelligent person, and when I needed you the most, you stayed right with me. You are my true parents and always will be. I am so sorry that I spoke to you in that manner. My anger took over my mind. I will never abandon you because you saved me from a life that would probably have not been pleasing."

Richard's eyes were glossy from tears, and in a strained voice, he leaned toward Marina and stretched out his hand to her. "I couldn't bear the thought of losing you. that's why we kept this secret. The moment we heard the news that you were about to be born, we left and traveled to get you. I loved you from the moment we were accepted as adoptees. When I held you for the first time, you gave me life."

"Now that this is out and in the open, we will try to help you find Julie. As we examine this situation, we can agree that she must have been the same age as you were when you had to live at The Fold. We don't know what she went through, but you should understand because you already lived through it. The set of circumstances with both mother and child living the same life years apart are very unusual. We will help you find Julie. I will call The Fold tomorrow and explain what happened and ask if we should make an appointment to visit and maybe get some help."

Margaret, with a mother's understanding heart, held on to Marina as they both rocked her like a child.

Marina held Richard's strong hand tightly, feeling the security she always felt from him.

"Thank you, Dad. All I want is to know the truth of why she gave me up. I would like to just look at her to see if I resemble her. I want to ask her questions like about my father. What was my father like, what does she look like, and do I resemble him also? Most importantly, did he leave her just like Jeff left me?"

"You have all legitimate questions that should be answered. When we first took you home and held you, we were thinking the same as you. We often wondered what ever happened to this young girl and what was the situation that made her leave you. We hoped that she made a good life for herself." Her mother searched Marina's eyes for comfort as she explained her feelings for Julie.

"Mom, could it be that she ran away from this truth, not wanting to ever relive these memories, which I understand since I have done the same to Seton? Maybe someday Seton to will find out about her adoption and search for me. What do you think about that?"

Mother answered. "Marina, anything is possible. Look at us here now. Who would have ever thought that we would be working together in a search for loved ones."

Then Marina's father spoke with a tender look in his eyes and with a soft tone to give comfort and counsel to his daughter.

"Just remember, if we do contact her, she will either accept or shun the idea. Either way, you have to ready yourself for her decision." Richard kept his eyes directly and seriously on Marina as he spoke with her.

"Yes, Dad, thank you for all this advice, and I want you both to know that through this I have learned to forgive. I forgive her for whatever reason she had to leave me, but I am thankful that the right parents came along and adopted me into this beautiful family."

"My dear, true love is endless in all different relationships. Nothing can separate us. After all, we are like eggs in a nest, hatching and growing together." Margaret lovingly sighed in relief, as if deflating the tension that was lifted.

In an instance they reached for her, holding her tightly, telling her how much they love her and will never leave her.

Marina went back to her room with the documents and just kept reading the letter and notes over and over. She held her head as she struggled to reread the letter and notes, choking out the tightness in her throat.

I hope I'm not about to find out any more bad news, she thought to herself as a chill shot through her body. *I'm adopted from The Fold, and my child has been adopted from the same. This is like a circle, not ending until this incident is brought to the surface.*

I need to talk to Michael and show him my adoption papers. But I'm not ready to talk about Seton. This is all so overwhelming for me.

That evening she arrived at Michael's door, and before she rang the doorbell, she noticed the grey color of his door was slightly blemished. It became a vision in her thoughts to think almost symbolically, as though it separated them from their future existence.

Why do I feel this way? It's not true, must be because this adoption paper made me feel separated from my parents; now I'm thinking the same for Michael. I'm becoming so emotional, she thought. Then a cold chill again ran through her body.

As Michael opened the door, he saw her cold, pallid skin and tried to sooth her as he brought her to sit on his sofa.

"What is wrong? Your appearance is upsetting to me. Something terrible has happened. Please, Marina, what is it?"

Her mouth felt dry, and with a choked voice, she whispered, "I want to just block out my whole life, which I just found out has been kept a secret from me until now! I can't explain it all. The only way is for you to read these two documents then tell me what you think."

Michael sat, focused on the papers, as his hand brushed over his forehead and kept a steady hold on his head, remaining silent and expressionless for a while. He rose to a standing position and walked over to the window and continued to stare out.

"I don't know what to say at this moment. This is an unforeseen circumstance. Let me gather my thoughts, just give me a few minutes. I feel like a storm just hit me!"

Although seemingly a dark situation, Michael was insightful to her emotions. He turned as if he made a discovery, quick like lightening, he scooped her up in his arms in such a way that she seemed weightless, and then together they fell into his sofa. Her hair looked wild as the jungle, and as he moved her hair behind her ear, he sensed her emotional pain. He held her tightly.

His eyes are so different in moments that are serious, compassionate; I want to stay in this moment. I can read his unspoken language in his eyes, she thought.

"We are in this together. On the edge of truth falling in deep, we can complete this puzzle. Isn't it better that you found this out now before we have to spend time on our wedding arrangements? This has to be taken care of first, and be thankful for the love from your adoptive parents. I'm proud of how they raised you and what you have become. They are your true parents who would give up their own lives for you."

"Oh, Michael, my eyes have been covered as if I have been looking through pink eyeglasses. Even so, I do appreciate the beautiful, loving family I have and what they have done for me. At first, I wasn't sure if I wanted to go down this uncertain road because I don't know what I will find. After spending these last few hours soul-searching, I decided to allow my soul to search and lead me to her."

Michael then examined the birth certificates and explained to her what she should do.

"It says here Canada—that's a long travel from here, so you need to go with your parents as soon as possible and make arrangements and do some investigating. Your parents know who you are, and they are half of your life. Revealing Julie's identity, you will find what constitutes your own individuality, and you will become whole."

Guilt trickled through her body, darkening her eyes, hiding the secret of the child she gave away for adoption. She swallowed hard from the mental duress, thinking of not revealing the truth of both she and Julie and leaving a part of their hearts behind at The Fold. Collecting herself, she decided it was time to go home and pack her things. She would travel to Canada, back to The Fold, her life revolving like a circle back to Seton.

CHAPTER 12

Within the following week, they were on their way to The Fold. Following a familiar course and an identical ride but carrying different conditions with a mission in mind, she traveled with her parents and with Laurie at her side again. Would the true information be revealed about her mother? Hidden in her thoughts, maybe somehow she could even find some information about Seton.

Passing by unchanged scenery, the corrals for horses were kept up; the long narrow stretch of unpaved road remained the same. As they drove closer to the end of the road, solid and undamaged was the sign with an arrow pointing for the direction to The Fold. Her parents walked ahead swiftly, but Marina and Laurie lingered behind a little. Marina, looking over to her right, saw the sea; the rocks jetting out and the scent filled her with the memories of her stay there. She pointed out to Laurie where she remembered where she fell when pregnant with Seton.

"Laurie, do you think I resemble Julie? There must be a reason why I am back at this place. I'll find her, and I'll find Seton. I know it for sure. Could it be that Julie also sat on the same boulders composing and writing her notes when when she was pregnant with me? Then I think of little Seton, who adopted her? Is she all right?"

"Marina, please calm down. You have so many unanswered questions. Please prepare yourself in case some cannot be answered. I do believe there is a reason for everything that happens in our lives. This is really an unusual case of two mothers living here at separate times and leaving their babies behind, and now a possibility of finding one of them. What a story Marina! And someday either you or I will write about it."

Laurie held Marina, arm in arm as they walked up to the front of the pavilion.

"Hasn't changed much, this old house, still strong and sturdy, even the flowers are in a beautiful bloom and probably as old as the house. The view is still clear from this porch, seems like time stands still here." Marina felt the sea in her heart and the waves running through her body as she indulged in recollection of the past.

They stepped inside to the greeting room where the mountainous windows were flooded with sunlight revealing sparkles throughout from the hanging prism. The cutting angles from the panes of glass allowed the natural light through in sun patterns.

"I see the antique desk is still in the same position in the corner. I remember my parents sat there with the director. She must be an antique to by now."

While Marina and Laurie both were giggling like two little girls, they were interrupted by a hush from her parents, as the director walked into the room.

She walked over to Marina with arms wide open and tenderly hugged her.

"I was happy to receive your mother's call about your visit back here to The Fold. Some girls do come back for just a visit and some in hopes to find out some private information. You have grown to a beautiful young woman and I am so happy that you are here with your adoptive parents. Even though I understand you found out in an odd way, but these things do happen and maybe for the best. Let's take a seat here and relax with some tea and I tell you what I can."

She hasn't changed so much, just a few wrinkles around the corners of her mouth, and her voice remains the same, but she seems gentler, she thought.

"I have a million questions that have to be answered. We need to know where to start. That is why we are here, and we need your help. Here are the letters we found that were written by Julie. Does this writing sound like her? Do you think she is curious enough to contact you in order to find me? Has she ever even tried?"

The director calmed Marina down and began to answer some questions.

"Your life story started here at The Fold, with a young couple longing for a child and contacting us in hopes of being qualified to adopt a baby of their own. This couple sat right here, who traveled so far because they loved you before you were born and before they saw you. They are called adoptive parents, to take by choice into a family relationship. Traveling with you back here to find your biological mother proves they are your true parents. With that said, you must know that when it comes to an adoption request, we remain very austere in who we choose for the child. Our background check indicated that your parents were very suitable to adopt you. From what they told me on the last phone call, about your completed studies only proves you have had a well-balanced life with them. I am glad we accepted their application and interview to adopt you."

"Oh yes, I agree wholeheartedly, and I know without a shadow of a doubt they love me for sure. I love every minute of memories they have built with me. That's why I would have never suspected this adoption. The other half of this trip is because since I have become a mother and had to give away my baby here at The Fold, I also can relate to Julie and the love of a biological mother during her teenage life. She doesn't know that we share the same situation. I have to reach her and let her know we are in the same predicament."

Marina's heart hit her chest so hard she thought everyone could hear it.

"I can tell you that most of the stories repeat for many of the young girls as you. I remember your biological mother. She was the same age as you were when you came here. She was in the same situation as you were, unable to raise you, being so young and confused. She wanted a good education, yet she didn't want to give you up. But you can see she made the right decision for you. She trusted The Fold, and rightly so, that we would put you in the right family."

"I know everything is confidential but please tell me more about my mother. Is there any indication as to where she might have gone from here? What did she look like, and what happened when she actually gave me away? Also, if you don't mind, what would you be allowed to share with me about Seton? Just so when I leave here, I can keep more information about them both in my heart. I do understand now that I may never find either one, or they may never find me."

The director looked straight and steady into Marina's eyes, with a willingness to be truthful yet not to divulge another's confidence. With a silvery voice, she began to explain in detail the reasons for secrecy and how to expand her search.

"Once a baby leaves here as you found on your birth certificate, a new one is issued with a new name. This has to be done in order to protect the innocence of the child and for the privacy of the mother. I have lived here as the director for many years and have seen so many young girls come and go. I have always made sure once the babies were adopted, their privacy was protected."

She sat, tapping her desk in thought, then decided to continue with some information.

"I was here when you were born, and I witnessed your birthing to Seton when you returned here to give birth. I have to say, this has never happened before. We do not know the whereabouts of the birthing mothers, sometimes the mothers have their names changed so they can move on to a new life knowing their child is safe."

The director blinked back tears as the conversation became more emotionally difficult, not wanting to damage her feelings. With empathy for her misfortune and with sensitivity in her voice, she carefully gave more information. She then left the room abruptly and returned with a round mirror on a long handle.

"Here, take a look in this mirror. This is your mother."

As Marina looked into the mirror, she realized the reflection was an image of her mother and her child, Seton.

"I understand now, and I see my daughter in this mirror besides my mother. What you're saying is, she has my red hair and my blue eyes."

"Yes, Marina, your mother was a beautiful young girl. I remember her long red hair and skin as fair as a princess with tiny freckles running across her nose. Just look in the mirror, and you will see her. I can tell you that as I look at you, I see her. You have her smile and bright-blue eyes as her. She enjoyed keeping a notebook and writing, although she never shared any of her writings. I'm sure she was talented. She didn't stay here on the grounds as you did. She said she was continuing her education elsewhere."

"Through this mirror, I have found my identity and my child. From grandmother to child, we definitely resemble each other." Marina held the mirror close to her chest as if holding her child.

"As for Seton, you know her name was changed, but that was done after they brought her home, the same as with you. Unless she finds her original birth certificate as you did, she will never know. I can tell you the parents came from a southern state, that I do remember, but southern where, that I do not remember. The records of all births here at The Fold are automatically sent to the state of the adoptee parents. Your cousin did a great job in exposing the truth by going to the registrar's office. But we do not know which state the couple brought Seton only because of a fire in the main office, which destroyed hundreds of files we had. So I have no way of accessing any sealed records that were originally sent out. Since you resemble your mother, I'm sure Seton resembles you. I hope that with the little information I was able to supply for you will in some way this will help you on your search for both mother and child."

Despair flashed across her face, then she leaned on her father's shoulder; he held her and patted on her head. She felt the comfort of home in his loving arms with the old scent of his cigar that sat tucked in his suit jacket pocket, making its way to her nostrils, reminding her that this was her family.

"I understand what you're saying, and I am grateful for the description of my mother and trust you with the knowledge of Seton's private life now. I am understanding more of the process of adoption. I need a little quiet time now, and since I love the atmosphere of The Fold and its surroundings, I would like to just walk around the grounds for a while."

"Of course, Marina, but on another note, you can start your search by contacting the clerk in the southern counties until you find her. Then be careful not to interfere with the privacy of that family."

The director invited her parents and Laurie to stay with her and enjoy more tea and biscuits in the living room. They all agreed, enjoying her pleasant conversation as her father admired all the antiques that he remembered from the long time ago when he first brought Marina there.

The grassy path remained the same over the years, leaving her imprint as her feet fell softly on the earth. She walked closer to the sea, and she could taste it spraying over her lips. With each step, she wondered if she stepped onto Julie's footprints she left behind so long ago. She found the boulders and driftwood not affected by the passage of time as she stepped into the shoreline. The broken driftwood swirled around her foot as its ridges nicked her ankle. She remembered the kicks of life she felt while finding comfort in the waves. Would Julie be too old now or maybe deceased? Would she herself pass away before ever finding her own child? An unknown gust of cold wind swept through her as she thought of her resemblance to Julie and maybe to her daughter, Seton, and how their paths would never meet.

Her hands rested on her empty, nonlife belly, then in a lamentation cry, almost demanded out over the water to Seton and in a pain-filled wailing.

"Seton, what have I done? this emptiness of my heart and womb is a never-ending restlessness. Come back to me. Hear my cry. My love for you has not been broken. I want you back in my arms/ I want you back inside me, where you would be safe and only mine again."

The wind snatched her words away, blowing stronger and pulling her tears across her cheeks. There was a wave of supernatural feeling as though something left her, something died. As the waves crashed, she heard a babies cry, or was it the sound of the seagull? Looking upward to the sky, asking the whipping of the wind to bring her up and away, she fell to her knees, pounding the wet shoreline and rocks, digging, looking, searching for an unknown, hidden treasure.

As she began to rise on her feet while watching the waves, it formed a curved shape, like hands beckoning and pulling her; she felt an urgency to go to the sea, to walk into it and never return.

"Yes, I am drawn to you, my friend. The sea is my friend."

A week passed, and everyone resumed as usual in their lives: Laurie back to work, Michael left for Tennessee, and Marina back at The Post.

Stumbling through this week of work is like living in a desert waste-land fighting against a sandstorm. My mind keeps repeating Cinderella, then Julie, now Cynthia. Really, who am I? she thought.

"We will get some answers soon, Marina. My lawyer friends are helping with some of the few facts we gave them. Together they should be able to unearth some information leading to the locations of both Julie and Seton."

"Thanks, Laurie. You're always by my side. If I ever have children, I will definitely name one of them after you."

"Well, I hope one of them is a girl! You can't name a son Laurie," Laurie answered jokingly to lighten the mood.

"Oh, thanks for the joking, I sure need it. It's been a while since I last spoke to Michael about the findings from The Fold. I'll give him a call now before he leaves for his visit to his parents. I understand he wants some alone time with them, and I guess he figures I'm tired from the trip back, but I don't understand why he didn't invite me?"

Marina felt excluded and rejected, but would not show her feelings to Michael when she called, but she hoped to find something in this voice.

"Michael, my quest for information took longer than expected. So sorry I didn't keep in touch while in Canada. I miss you so much and was hoping to spend quality time with you."

"Marina, I'm just glad you're home safe, and with the little information you received, I believe you will find something. I know Laurie is helping, but if you need my help, I'm here for you. I have missed you so much, but it seems our situations and timing has over-lapped. We will definitely make it up when I get back. I am leaving now for the airport, I will be in Tennessee tonight. I will call you when I settle in. Love you and miss you already."

"It's okay, Michael. I totally understand. Thank you for your emotional support in all that I have been going through with this new adoption findings. I love you. Come back quick!"

Michael didn't share with Marina his true feeling, as he had some kind of suspicion about her adoption; so he made copies of the birth certificates to bring to his parents to see if they had any advice for him. He couldn't free himself from this troublesome news of Marina being adopted; it left him with uneasy feelings and concerns about her unknown lineage of her true culture and health issues.

CHAPTER 13

Michael arrived at his parents' home and was made comfortable in his old room.

The rich aroma of something delicious cooking on the stove reached his nose with a memory of one of his mom's delightful dinner recipes. He decided it was time to go downstairs and show them the birth certificates.

"Where is Cordelia now? I saw her briefly when I arrived, and now she disappeared," Michael laughed as he sat at the kitchen table.

"She is busy outside in the backyard running to feed the swans and to climb up onto her favorite tree. I just can't keep her down, so much energy." Lenora chuckled while stirring her recipe in a big pot on the stove.

"Mom, Dad, please sit down a minute before she comes back, I have to show you something important." Michael sat with a long and mournful face.

Joseph read aloud to his wife what was written on the paper.

"Marina is Cinderella? Her biological mother is a Julie Gagnon, and father unknown. Adopted by Richard and Margaret Martin? Why, this is a shock! She was adopted!"

"This is so serious, Michael. She must be in shock. What is going to happen now?"

"Mom, she was in dire need. This situation put her in great fear and worry. I did the best to calm her down. It was so hard for her with her parents, but as families should, they bonded together even more and went together to a place called The Fold where she was adopted. Marina retained some information about her biological

113

mother. With that. her cousin Laurie, also a lawyer, has her team working on it. So do I."

"We will try and help with this puzzle as much as we can to find a solution for poor Marina. We have a few family court lawyers in our church. We can give one of them a call and show these copies. I know this is a shock for her, but now she needs to find her bio mother and grandparents if they are still alive."

"I know, Mom. I know her adopted parents must feel hurt, but they are such decent people to take her all the way to this place, The Fold, for information. They have truly shown their love for her. Most importantly, I think it's crucial to find out her background, like what is her real heritage. To find out important facts that will help her to understand just who she is."

"Yes, son, and what family traits does she carry, like illnesses. In our family, my father suffered from high blood pressure, so I inherited that. Thanks to your mom, she makes sure I have the best diet. She's keeping me alive!" His father tried to ease the conversation.

"Well, I feel like I need to release some mental pressure, so I'll go out to the backyard and find my little Cordelia. All I have to do is hear her little voice and watch her animated gestures, and I will feel the weight of the world disappear." Michael rushed to the back door to find his little sister.

"She certainly brought her own exuberance to this family, and we are all thankful for this little surprise package," Joseph called out as Michael went to the door.

When Michael left, his parents ran in urgency to find the papers they hid years ago. Hastily they searched in the untidy drawers of their dressers until they found the key that would open the old hope chest that was a wedding gift so long ago. With a couple of clicks, it opened, and Dad pushed around to the bottom under tablecloths, bedsheets and blankets, and old jewelry.

Hidden under mounds of Lenora's treasurers was a narrow, long, brown box. With trembling hands, he raised up the box, glancing up with fleeting eyes to his wife, already knowing what they were about to read. She hesitantly, almost timidly, took the box and delicately pushed her one finger on a panel, which then opened a secret compartment. Another key was hidden inside for her to open the brown box, which had not been touched since the birth of Cordelia. They opened it together and found Cordelia's two birth certificates. Both hoped that their suspicion was wrong, for it has been years since they even looked at the names on the papers. As they opened the first document, they found it to be the original one that they once thought of destroying:

Child: Seton Cynthia Martin. Born: December 22, 1967.
Mother: Marina Cynthia Martin. Father: Unknown.

Child: Cordelia Cynthia Smith. Born: December 22, 1967.
Mother: Lenora R. Smith. Father: Joseph M. Smith.

Putting the birth certificates side by side, they knew that this Marina who was supposed to be their future daughter-in-law was the mother of their adopted child, Cordelia. With this unveiling truth, how could they tell their little girl of her adoption, and the one she looked up to as her new big sister, that she was actually her real mother? And their son—how do they explain all this confusion to Michael?

"Lenora, it is probably the right time to tell Michael. This is like a spiderweb, spreading out in all different directions and not so beautiful. This can't be hidden any longer, plus I feel this is going to be an explosion. Especially if Marina never told Michael she had a child."

"Joseph, this is unbelievable. There must be a strange reason why this was all put together in this family. It's not a web. Its thick dust being stirred up with no windows to escape. It's going to penetrate our lungs. I can't even breathe now." Lenora took on a pale look, like whitewash, and crumbled in Joseph's arms.

When Lenora and Joseph first met Marina, her name kept ringing in their heads as they discussed how Cordelia had a small resemblance to her. In their private conversations, they never thought to check the birth certificates and never cared to since all time has passed, and Cordelia belonged to them. Now all suspicions were gone, for they realized Marina was the mother of their adopted child.

They became distraught over the truth like a terminal illness came over them. Feeling weak, she held her hand over her heart, feeling as if her heartbeats would break her ribs. He quickly sat her down and helped her to breathe.

"We will tell Michael soon before they make the wedding arrangements. This cannot remain a secret now that we have met Cordelia's real mother. This is going to be devastating to Michael, how this has turned into a winding circle. Cordelia cannot know of this until all is settled with Michael and Marina. First of all, Cordelia is too young to have to go through all these changes now. One thing at a time, and we will get through this. We have to help Marina and her parents to understand all this," Joseph choked out the words in his own distress.

"No, this can't be happening. She can't take my baby away from me."

Lenora screamed as if ice chips were poured down her back, repeating it over and over until she felt so limp in his arms.

Michael still hunted for Cordelia in the backyard, wondering where she hid, and his yells echoed between the trees.

"Cordelia, come on out from hiding. It's too quiet out here without you. Okay, look out, I'm coming to get you!" Michael kept yelling out through the yard, cupping his hands over his mouth like a microphone.

Scouting the back acreage, he saw the old willow tree, but no little figure near or on it. In his long walk, he reflected on the situation about Marina and how this would affect his life. His slow easy pace became faster with longer strides as he began to wonder where Cordelia was. She must be hiding in that shed again with the ducks.

As he passed the pond, he climbed up the shed ramp, and it was empty, so he jumped off and started a fast pace toward the tree. He thought this was not unusual to find her somewhere else on the property. As he drew closer to the tree, he saw something dark on the bottom of the tree, looking like a bag of something; he started with a quicker pace.

Screaming her name and running faster, he realized it was his little sister, but there was no movement. Standing over her in fear, he knelt down and turned her over, removing the dirt and leaves from her face. He placed his finger over her neck and found a slight pulse. In his despair, he cried a loud, piercing cry, screaming for help. Quickly picking her up, he began to run with her body drooping in his arms until he bolted through the back door. Trying to scream out for help while fighting for his breath, they could hear him plummet to the floor from upstairs. His parents dropped everything and ran downstairs as they entered the kitchen, finding him crying over her body.

Joseph mechanically dialed the phone with a cracking voice. As tremors moved through his body, he finally got the message out.

"Operator, quick. I need an ambulance. My daughter is unconscious."

Crying out in a harsh, dusty voice, Lenora frantically grasped onto Michael's shirt, pulling persistently, as if pulling him for help.

"Revive her, Michael. Do something. Cordelia, wake up."

Lenora's voice begins to crack, then Joseph struggled to pull her off Michael as she became limp, almost in a paralyzed state.

All that could be heard from across the field was their long, pain-filled wailing like a howling wind. A wave of blackbirds and crows perched on the back porch, simultaneously crying with their grating coos of mournful cries.

That night at the hospital they were told to stay for a while in the waiting room just outside the hallway where Cordelia was placed in her room. The room was as dark as the deep black-and-blue rug Michael paced upon as though making a path. His parents sat fastened to their seat, staring, watching each step he made, almost inviting them to share in the nervous walk. A nurse walked in, dressed in glaring white, matching the sterile environment, and in a monotone voice, addressed them, "You can follow me now, but do not make any loud noises, just talk softly with her."

Feeling lifeless, they followed the nurse to the room. As they entered the door, the sight of Cordelia was a look of loss. Their lives were now thrown into chaos, knowing this didn't resemble Cordelia.

"Oh god, no! Don't let this be true. Give her life again. As I lay over her, give her breath. She's there, just lying like a cold, wet sand.

Oh god, please pour life into her now," Lenora cried out a mother's prayer as she stared, waiting for a movement of her little body.

They all surrounded her bed, emotionless, waiting for a word from the doctor.

The doctor walked in and looked at each face, deciding what to say, then called Michael out of the room and into the hallway.

"Michael, listen to me carefully. She could be permanently disabled. If her breathing does not become unassisted, she will die. She has a fractured neck, collapsed lung, and bad head injury. After my neurologic examination, she is unresponsive, and there are motor abnormalities. The frontal lobe is at immobility stage. At this point, she remains catatonia."

The doctor's words were as cold and lifeless as the sterile hospital. All Michael could do was set his eyes on the steel bars that covered the glass windows. Speechlessness with waves of nausea showed in Michael's face.

The doctor sat him in a nearby chair in the hallway and tried to calm him; finally, Michael was able to listen.

"You should probably make arrangements now for her, since I believe there will not be much time left. There are important decisions to make, and you are your parents' helper now." The doctor's tone with his words was serious and precise but somewhat distant in a professional way.

"I know. I will. First, I want to be with her now for a while, and I have to explain to my parents, then I'll go see my pastor." Michael held back his emotions of rage and grief while trying to absorb all that the doctor told him.

The room was silent with only the sound of her soft, labored breathing as the hissing of the ventilator conveyed its hope to prolong life. Lenora placed her hand over Cordelia's while silently praying for a sign of life.

"Inert she lays as if only sleeping, my little girl, she has to wake up."

Her father stood frozen, resting his hand on her foot, praying for some kind of movement of life.

Michael walked back into the room and saw that nothing medically will change for Cordelia. His parents with a blank look of hopelessness gazed up as Michael rubbed his brow and came closer to the bed. His voice cracked with anguish, asking them to please let him be alone with her for a moment.

He placed his hands on her head and faced upward to the sky, pleading to God.

"Please take me instead, even though I am not worthy to be with you now. Let's make an exchange of lives. I'm not even worthy to live. She is just an innocent child. Please let her live."

Then Michael leaned over Cordelia, facing her and holding her face in his palms.

"Oh, Cordelia, I can't live without you. You're my lifeline to this unfaithful world. Hear me, little sister, and don't take away the only sunshine I know of. This world needs you. Please listen to me, hear me, and come back."

Like chipping flint cracking the walls, Michael's words forced over the sound of the machine. Lifting himself from her bed to leave her room, he watched as the machine pushed through her airways with false sounds of life.

With weak and shallow breath, Michael walked to his parents and held their hands tightly.

"Mom, I want to see our pastor now. I need to talk to him about all that's going on here. I think he should know. He will probably come back with me to see Cordelia. I will return as soon as possible. do not leave her side for a minute."

They returned to the room with hands clasped in prayer as they pressed their lips to her forehead, waiting for a positive reaction. Their tears fell onto her face, hoping that she might even feel something and turn toward them to even blink once.

That afternoon, Michael sat waiting for Pastor John in his office in the rear of the church. His eyes locked into the colorful stained-glass figure of St. Michael etched in the window across the room.

Where are you now St. Michael that Cordelia needs you? he thought.

Just then, Pastor John walked in and sat down next to Michael. He was tall in appearance, but gentle in manner, a quiet listener, always ready to be of help to anyone in his congregation. He was not only a pastor to Michael's family, but a constant friend over the years. He was considered a family member, especially for any holiday occasion. He remembered holding Michael at his baptism, and now he sat with the child that became a man.

"When I got your call at the parsonage, I just fell to my knees. I can't believe this is happening. Please fill me in what the doctor has to say."

With quivering breaths, Michael proceeded to explain what happened.

"When I found her, she was lifeless. I think at that moment, I knew she was gone. But the little hope I had was that I was wrong. Now the doctor said to make the arrangements."

Pastor John tried to hold back his emotions by just nodding while holding his breath as Michael talked.

"Michael, I have been like an uncle to her. I held her at her christening, I watched her grow. I don't know why this happened. I have no answers, and I feel like I'm losing a little sister also. This is going to be very hard for all of us. Such an unexpected tragedy."

As Michael talked, Pastor's mind became filled with images of little Cordelia; all the joy she brought to him and this family flashed through his mind.

Michael's long hard-exhaled breath brought Pastor back to their conversation. With teary eyes, leaning forward arms clutching, he finally glanced up toward Michael and exhaled as if holding his breath through the whole conversation.

"I will make all the necessary arrangements. You and your family will not have to deal with anything. Just stay by her side. I will meet you in the hospital within a couple of hours. Go back to the hospital and stay with her and your parents until I get there."

With blurred eyesight and tears welling up, Michael left, knowing at least he would not have to deal with the horror of funeral arrangements. He managed to drive back to the hospital, feeling his body drained from the morning terror and what he took care of through the day.

Pastor, sitting alone in his office, thought back to the day Cordelia came home from The Fold. He was there to greet Lenora and Joseph and their new adopted daughter. He also helped with the new birth certificate from the lawyer in his congregation. He has carried this secret in his heart for years and now believed it was time to share this with Michael when the time was right.

He knelt down by his sofa and gazed upward in prayer for her, and then as if she were in the room, he spoke to her, "Little Cordelia, how you filled our lives with joy and love. you can't leave us now."

Pastor knelt by his sofa and pleaded for her life as his cries echoed only in his ears.

On Michael's return to the hospital, he ran straight to Cordelia's room and approached his parents.

"Mom, Dad, please sit here. I have to explain to you what the doctor told me."

Michael began to inform them of the doctor's diagnosis and why he had to meet with the pastor. When he finished explaining, he held his parents tightly as they seemed weak in his arms. Lenora went into shock and fell to the floor. Joseph barely had the strength to help Michael pick her up and place her back onto the chair. Everything was a blur to him, an endless swirl out of existence for him.

"Michael, this is one of shock and horror for us all. We, your mother and I, did not expect this news. We have to get back to Cordelia's bed side."

"Michael, I'm ok now. I have to be with her. Help me walk back in her room."

"I know, Mom, Pastor is taking care of everything. He said don't worry, do nothing, just stay here. He is on his way. Also, I think Marina should know about this. I have been out of touch with her, and she has also been dealing with her adoption issues. I'll go home and call her now and make arrangements for her to fly in, but first, I want to spend time with Cordelia."

"Yes, Michael, that is a good idea. She should know about this, have her and her parents come to our home. We all will need comforting."

Lenora's words were cold and detached, just a robotic sound, and then she turned and went back into Cordelia's room.

Marina, driven by her own quest for the truth of her own discovery, became so absorbed she forgot to keep in touch with Michael. At the same moment, when she finally sat to think of everything that was going on in her life, she then remembered Michael; and at that moment, the phone rang.

"Michael, I am so sorry for not keeping in touch with you. I have so much to share with you about my visit to The Fold. It has taken this long to get my information."

Michael slouched in the chair, gripping the phone tightly as he tried to control his voice.

With steady breaths he began to silence her by breaking into her conversation, "Please listen to me carefully, Marina. Something important you need to know. Cordelia is in the hospital. She fell off the willow tree and was unconscious. You need to fly in. I want you to be here for her. I'll arrange your flight, and I will also include your parents. I am so sorry that I have to tell you this over the phone, but we need you here."

The room began to fade as Marina dropped the phone and screamed for her mother, forgetting Michael was still on the phone. Her parents came running in and caught her as she sank down on her bed. Her father took the phone, then wide-eyed and twisted mouth, he hung up. Feeling such grief and mental suffering, they all just lay there together, not able to move, losing track of time. They remained holding Marina as she lay slump in a fetal position through the night.

Michael felt a chilly sensation as he entered the room; there was an inability for anyone to speak.

"It's sunset, Cordelia. Can you feel the dim twilight shadow covering you? Can you feel the warmth of my hands, little sister?"

A vacant look covered her little face as he delicately held her hands together in prayer, feeling the cold blood pumping through her veins. Her lips began to turn a pale white; he lifted his hand to gently brush her hair away from her forehead, waiting for some type of movement from her long eyelashes, but not even a flitter. He felt the room spinning, moving too quickly. He had to move away. There were no words left to speak; not even a word of comfort could be formed in anyone's mind.

That night gave its message across the sky as its darkness entered the room with the gloom of a nightmare. Then a divine ray passed over Cordelia like a silver moonbeam giving a flash of light to the dark room. There was an illumination over her head, like a morning light, almost metallic. Then Cordelia's face began to glow, and the sound of wind carried through the room, robbing them of the light, leaving them in the blackness of despondency.

CHAPTER 14

They didn't remember how they found their way home that night. A heavy cloud covered their eyes from the impact of watching the respirator being removed and the sound of Cordelia taking her last breath. The silence all around them was as thick as the night from such a harrowing experience. A spirit of weariness settled in their hearts as they walked into the house. Michael sat at the kitchen table with his head drooping in his hands, eyes drifting shut and bloodshot looks up at his mom. Dark circles under her eyes, and his heart broke. He looked to his dad sagging in the chair with hands hanging limply, beginning to feel helpless toward them. Michael began to speak in a dusty voice, as if a noose was around his neck.

"Mom, Marina's flight is tonight. I have to go pick her up at the airport. Last I spoke to her, Cordelia was in the hospital. You should come with me when I tell her this bad news. Her parents will be with her."

With glazed over eyes and a distant look she responded with a lack of facial expression.

"Of course, Michael. I wouldn't want her to hear this and not be able to be comforted. This is not easy for anyone."

She continued to sit at the table, becoming despondent, losing track of the conversation, and not being able to believe what just happened.

Joseph sat in a heavy cloud of anger and self-blame and began striking his fists onto the top of the table, and with a raging voice, he said, "It's that damn tree. I gave her to much freedom. I should not have allowed her to go that far into the property."

"No, I should have been more watchful. from my kitchen window, I can see her. I trusted her surroundings too much," she said, holding her shaking head and feeling so alone like a victim held prisoner to her thoughts.

"Well then, I'm to blame also. I should have come around more often. It would have given her something to look forward to, not just the birds, the swans, and the tree!"

The noisy quarrel began and continued like a rope unraveling until it reached the end, then they stopped and sat on the sofa, holding each other in desperation. Michael went into the small office his dad kept for bills and anything anyone wanted to file away. He sat in his dad's leather office chair and just looked around. There were pictures of Cordelia at her dance recital, pictures of the family at the church BBQ.

Emotionless, he sat with skin tone matching the gray painted walls, and with a blank stare in absolute silence, he wished he could easily disappear within its color.

A week passed by, and Pastor John made sure all arrangements were made. He brought them lunch daily and sat with them nightly.

"I made all the necessary arrangements for the church service and for refreshments after the service to be held at the parsonage so as not for anyone to remain at the burial site. Your request that the burial will be under her weeping willow tree has been settled."

Pastor John towered over Lenora as he spoke, hoping his tears wouldn't reach her face.

"Yes, it was there where she lay beneath the tree and did her homework. She often sat on the largest extended branch to look out at the edge of the property, watching the horses and writing notes. She loved to write rhymes and verses. Imagine a little six-year-old writing about life." Her hand reached for Pastor's hand in an effort to reach for his comfort.

With a slight laugh, they said, "How could a little six-year-old write poetry?"

Lenora expressed it was the perfect spot for her to be buried over the hill.

"She will live and breathe life to her willow tree forever."

The morning of the funeral was a sunny day as the family sat on the back porch, watching the birds and waiting for their time to leave for the church.

"Mom, why is the sun shining so bright today on the worse day of our lives?" Michael said, biting his lip and fidgeting in his seat.

"I don't know, Michael. I don't know anything at this moment," she stuttered the answer with a flushed face, watching the birds flying on the great willow tree.

Richard and Margaret followed their daughter, Marina, out onto the deck to sit with them. Nervously, they all sat down.

Lenora sat with hunched posture and said with fixed eyes, speaking out into the yard, "We really should leave now. Pastor called, said everyone is arriving at the church."

All, staring into space like robots, rose from their seats and mechanically walked to the car.

The parsonage was filled with everyone from the church, including neighbors from miles away. There were plenty of food and desserts since each family brought their special dish. Continuous conversations went on about the beautiful eulogy Pastor gave for Cordelia.

"I share with you that as she is planted beneath her favorite tree, she has bloomed in heaven today. If all our love could have saved her, this sweet child would have never died, but God, in his mercy, wrapped her in his loving arms, for he needed another angel, and he chose her. Yes, we will mourn her loss, but she has no tears or pain anymore."

His tearful words about this unimaginable death ended with the praising words of her life lived here on earth and all the love and joy that came from her innocent heart.

In the crowded room, there were sounds of sobbing and yet laughter over the talks and sharing stories of the little cute things she did. Slowly the parsonage emptied, leaving the silent sound of loneliness. Fatigued and overwhelmed with the after scent of various ladies' and men's perfumes and the hours that just took place, the family decided it was time to go home.

"I will check up with you later, giving you some private time now, and then, of course, tomorrow please keep in touch and call me in between."

Then pastor held them one at a time, not wanting to let go, carrying their pain and his own.

The sky put on a show as the family sat on the back porch, watching the setting sun and rising moon. Even the deafening sounds of the crickets went undisturbed to their ears, as they were very absorbed by the loud storm of thoughts in their mind of this dark day. A soft gust of wind with a sweet scent of grass and leaves like flora blew by undetected. Lines of pain remain unconcealed and could not escape their faces.

"Too much property. I should have thought of that years ago. I thought this was a healthier life for her. I'm not sure this is where I can live any longer. Miles of property only gives me memories of her. I can't look out there anymore." Covering his eyes with one hand, with his other hand over his aching chest, Joseph struggled to get the words out.

"We will always have Cordelia with us now up over the hill. It will feel peaceful knowing she is still here on our property. Time will pass from the winter's frozen world to the sparrow's song of spring. she will always be with us," Lenora weakly answered with a sound of cotton stuck in her throat

Michael's voice made the sound of a slightly husky tone, as if gasping breath as he looked to where Cordelia showed him where she wanted her treehouse. "I never got to build her that tree house she wanted. Maybe if I did, she wouldn't have…" His words drifted off slowly, quietly, like one falling to sleep.

"Before it gets any darker, let's take a walk up over the hill and check on Cordelia," Lenora said with an unfocused gaze, pretending the child was still there, and became disengaged in their conversation, pushing her mental status in grief.

They all walked together on the evening dew-drenched grass in silence to the grave. Standing motionless over the freshly turned-over ground, as if waiting for her to appear, the backhoe equipment could be seen farther down away from where it just finished turning over the earth. Sweating beads on their foreheads and muscles quivering, they stood on the still-wet and muddy ground, reminding them of how they watched her little coffin being sent down under the ground.

"We will build a shrine here for her where the first flowers of spring will grow under her tree. She loved the birds and would sit here with crumbs of bread for them."

This traumatic event in their lives left them in numbness, grief, and shock that shifted to anger. Marina turned away from the fresh grave and looked toward the rising moon, staring at the translucent light.

She thought, *Nothing weeps like a willow. I want to make this my home and never leave, and my connection to her is strong as if we are one.*

The next morning, they were startled by a loud, crashing sound, thinking the house was falling down. They all ran out to see Joseph out by the shed with a sledgehammer in his hand. As they all started running toward him, they saw him breaking down the shed in anger. With each strong pounding of the hammer, he cursed the shed and the ground he built it on.

"Everything has to go, down with the shed. I'll drain the pond, and I'm selling all this extra property. No more animals, no more birds, no shed!"

Sweat poured from his head as the veins popped out in his neck while his mind went into hysteria.

"Dad, stop, please. Oh god, you're killing yourself. This is not the answer to your pain," said Michael.

Michael felt like his was losing his hold on his father's strong body. Finally, Marina's dad stepped in and grabbed him by the waist, and they all fell to the ground.

Marina's hands, arms, and head became like tremors as she reached for him.

She said, "Dad, please talk to Joseph. This is unhealthy."

"Joseph, please listen to us. This is so painful, we all feel it, and your actions can bring on a heart attack. Pick him up and bring him back into the house," Marina cried to him and suddenly felt a surge of strength.

With slow movements, they helped him to his feet, not letting go of him. They locked their arms, with him walking him like a zombie back into the house. Lenora gave him a sedative the doctor recommended to keep while going through this depression. Margaret helped to get him a glass of water, while Richard sat close by, making sure he was calming down.

"Dad, I'll take care of the property. Don't worry. Anything broken can easily be fixed. I'll fix it all up later. You just have to rest now. I don't want to lose you."

Lenora brought him to their room and made sure he rested and hoped he would fall asleep. She sat with steady eyes on him, feeling the emotional hurt he went through.

Time was swept away like a strong current of wind crashing and uprooting each agonizing day.

"Michael, everything has changed now. our wedding plans must be put on the back burner for a while. I can't think of not having her in our wedding party. My mind can't handle this. I feel like there is a hole in my heart."

"I feel the same, Marina. The wind brought a change in our lives. A whole new life-changing decision has been created. I need time to put my mind back into a normal state, and I need time to help my parents go through this."

"Absolutely. Do you feel my parents and I should leave now to give you personal time with them? I mean, I really don't want to. I want to stay here where I can still feel her."

"You're not leaving. You have all been so genuinely kind and helpful to us. You have to stay. It will help me to take care of all this property since Dad is not able to right now."

"Okay, Michael. My dad can help man-to-man with your father, and my mom is so gentle with your mom. She will be able to help her. I will try to be the strong shoulder for you, but I need you also. My mind feels very weak. We both suffer the same for Cordelia, but she was your blood, your only sister."

Alone in their room, Joseph and Lenora held the birth and death certificates in their hands together, crying and reminiscing the joys of her adoption and the pain of her death.

"It's time, Lenora, to talk to Marina and tell her the truth. It's been a month. I feel stronger now, and I don't want her to leave without knowing the truth. Although this is going to be more shocking and painful for her, I think she should be told as soon as we speak to the others so we, all together, can help her. I'll have our doctor on hand in case she needs a sedative."

Joseph placed the certificates down and held his wife's hands, giving her the warmth of comfort that she also needed.

"This is such a sensitive matter. I was thinking the same, but we have to talk to Michael first. This is going to give him a second shock. When we tell him his little sister was adopted while he was away at school is another disturbance, but when he finds out the woman he is going to marry is her mother is really going to be an upsetting experience for him." Lenora felt the emotional pain in her heart for herself and Marina.

"This is really a disturbing situation, since she never told him her secret. I believe it must have been so painful to give her baby up, and the death of her long-lost child who was unknowingly right in front of her will be pain in a greater degree for her."

Joseph understood a mother's heart as he watched his wife also suffer through this experience, and he felt his own weariness as he rubbed his brow and closed his eyes to think.

"I know, Joseph, but I think we should talk privately with Michael first. His reaction to this will be like dark clouds looming in. We have to be at his side as he needs to recover. That is why this should be discussed privately at Pastor's parsonage, especially since Pastor was here when Cordelia arrived. Then we can approach her parents and let them recover from this trauma so they can help us with Marina."

"Recovery time for all of us. None of this would have been revealed if..." His voice lowered and ended, trailing off into a hush, leaving them in soundlessness without the power of speech.

Lenora looked up toward the sky with her silent tears and held on to Joseph's hands and felt the comfortable warmth of love from him.

"Joseph, it's difficult to imagine her in a cold grave, no more cuddles and goodnight kisses. But my faith tells me our baby is safe up there. It's the only thought that gives me strength."

At the end of that week, arrangements were made to meet with Pastor and Michael. Joseph mentioned to Michael that Pastor would like him to accompany them to his office for a private session. Michael agreed, thinking it was time to have a counseling session about Cordelia.

There was a sudden drop in blood flow as he held on to the side of the pastor's sofa, and sharp breaths increased as he reached up a hand and clasped his throat. With a voice devoid of emotion and with heavy limbs, Michael rose from the sofa and walked to the window. His speech was slow as he forced the words out of his ridged mouth.

"Her outward appearance is so pleasant, but she concealed the truth from me. She doesn't trust me. She lied to me. Our relationship was originally based on truth and sharing, but now I feel like I'm living in a dream. She gave birth. She became a mother and gave her child away. How could this be? Her baby was my sister. I just can't accept or understand any of this! I feel so sick right now."

"Son, we are so sorry we never told you about Cordelia. We thought it didn't matter because you loved her so much. We will find out more about Marina's life through her parents and then Marina. I am sure that giving up her child was a very traumatic time in her life. When I gave birth to you, my life was reborn, but you were mine for life. Marina's life was different from ours. we don't know the particular as of yet."

"Why the big secret? Why camouflage something that could have been celebrated? I could have been a part of the adoption process. I was old enough to understand it's nothing to be embarrassed about. I am just as angry with you to."

Michael turned to them with a powerful word punch like glassy shards; he continued to pace and scream at everyone in the room.

"Must you turn over every stone, Michael? Is this your revenge? Your mother lost two babies, which is when your parents decided to adopt. Have mercy on them. Don't throw stones and cause more pain and chaos." Pastor's eyes glared as he spoke in a cold hard voice to Michael.

Michael's accusations became bitter and incriminating toward everyone in the room. Pastor was a quiet and peaceful man, but in defense of Joseph and Lenora, he became bitter toward Michael. Pastor's words hit hard like the rage of a volcano, then he walked over to the side of the room and leaned against the wall, with his fingertips gripping into the crevices of the windowpane, never wanting to show his anger or true feelings.

"Michael, this all seems to be something that was supposed to unravel through us for whatever reason. But isn't it peculiar that out of nowhere, you meet Marina and bring her into our family?"

Joseph was still in shock but his voice wanted to reach Michael's emotional pain and help him to understand the situation they were all in now.

"Dad, I just can't shake all this off my mind and body. I still feel like I'm in limbo."

"Michael, I've been your pastor all of your life, and I agree this is a very strange situation, but I agree with your father. This is a strange set of circumstances for all of us, but we will understand it all soon, I'm sure. It's like the whole situation was in lost pieces and are now finally being pieced together. There is definitely a reason for this."

Then Lenora, still with a distant look in her eyes, reached out and took Michael's hand, speaking in a soft tone to him, "Michael, let me remind you, we didn't want to lie to you about the adoption. But I lost two babies while being pregnant at six months. Pain seared through my abdomen, branding it with torment. Each pregnancy giving me false hope that traveled to my moods destroyed me. I began to wither, giving your father gloom. Finally, there was a spark of hope when we heard we could adopt. Your father and I felt new life, a new beginning, and a new family. So there were no lies from us. We just covered up the pain until Cordelia came."

The following day, Joseph, Lenora and Michael took Marina's parents, Richard and Margaret, back to the pastor's office to give them all the information.

"This feels like murder. The pain bores down in our souls, leaving it empty for the rest of our lives. Whenever I would go shopping and see a little girl, I would always wonder if she was my grandchild, carrying the guilt of having Marina give her up. Now I know who she was. I could have been holding her on my visit and not even know it."

Margaret, trying to make sense of all that has happened, could only show the pain in her watery eyes as she tried to massage the loud noise of pain from her head.

Richard, affected by the intensity of the conversation, could only nod in a slow movement as his words murmured off his tongue.

"Knowing that Marina would never see her daughter, and we would never see our biological granddaughter, was painful enough all these years, but this feels more tragic. Our love for that little one was our only connection, and we prayed that someday we would unite. Here we had the chance, and she left us, so the pain will always simmer beneath our hearts."

Margaret, sitting back with dull eyes and watching all the pieces begin to fit, spoke, bringing a message of love and hope in a lightened voice.

"There is no formula for healing grief. We four sit here and share a common ground now, and we are family. We are all in bereavement—Michael, with the confusion of his sister and Marina. We share our grief of losing Cordelia, but you Lenora and Richard, finding her biological mother is a true shock. In addition, Richard and I now find Cordelia, our granddaughter after her death. The past has come to disrupt the future, but it will not linger. We won't let it. Marina will need us now more than ever when we sit her down and reveal what we have found."

CHAPTER 15

That night, Pastor came to their home to sit with them as they explained to Marina exactly what happened. Paralyzed and feeling the darts of the enemy in a battlefield, Marina, with breaths sawing in and out, began trembling, and with a prolonged, high-pitched cry of pain, she fell to the floor. In long, loud, wailing cries, she felt the death of her life.

"Oh god, why did you take her from me a second time? She was here, right in my arms, and I didn't know. My baby! My child! I felt something when I held her, that baby scent. Oh my god, no, no, please tell me this is a dream!"

Her strength became stronger as she thrashed her body on the floor. Michael tried to pin her down with his body as everyone else tried to grasp her legs down, but she fought with physical blows with her fists in a powerful, vigorous struggle. Her adrenaline increased and caused a hysterical strength in extreme, overpowering them. In exhaustion they released their grip on her, and she ran out the back door.

Michael's mother sat on the floor in disbelief, weeping bitterly as her mouth quivered and her body gave a shudder.

"Leave her alone. This is how she will mourn."

Michael, sensing something is not right with Marina, rose to his feet and peered out the window.

"No, something beyond mourning. She has lost her mental faculties. We have to follow her. She's running to Cordelia's grave!"

There was a sudden cloudburst of heavy rainfall as they ran after her over the small hill; following the dark mud path in the torrent of rain, they saw her as she sank to her knees under the willow, her body hunched over. Ebony-colored crows flying overhead in a driving force became raucous, leading Michael's run. As they came closer, they saw her arms moving in a digging motion over the tiny grave. They found her scratching the earth with her nails, digging through the dark wet earth as it clumped around her hands to unearth what lay below.

As she sat at the tiny grave, she could not feel the damp mud under her. She couldn't feel rain that mingled with her sobbing of tears as she grasped the mud. She wailed with a piercing screeching sound, like the sound of a widow's lament, echoing and gouging out the heavy, cold clay soil, smearing her body with the wet mud and pushing it into her stomach.

"I'll save you, Seton. I'll bring you back to life. You belong back here in me. Go back. Come back to me. Oh god, no. Take me with you, Cordelia, Seton!"

In her ferocious aggressiveness, it gave Michael no choice but to slap her into consciousness, seize her by the waist with one arm, and with the other palm of his hand, gave her a strong slap across her cheek. Instantly her hysteria stopped, and she fell spiritless into his arms, and he carried her back to the house. The resounding thunder echoed her wails, which the torrent rain could not quiet her pain.

Like night watchmen, they took turns guarding her through the night until morning ended the rain. Her nightlong laments for Cordelia ended, and the morning sun moved over her eyes, waking her. She lay still in the bed with expressionless eyes fixed on Michael. He found her icy stare and total absence of facial expression disconcerting.

"Marina, please listen to me. You have to respond, and you have to talk to me. Show me you are okay."

Margaret walked into the room, wringing her hands then leaning over her daughter, softly stoking her hair.

"Marina, we are all here to help you. The doctor gave you a sedative last night, but it must have worn off by now. Please talk to me. I love you. I want to help."

Michael saw her face was still soft but tinged with sorrow, her gaze faraway, floating through an empty space, knowing where her thoughts have gone. Once inflamed with anger about her cover-up and now watching her wither away, his feelings turn to empathy, reminding himself he lost his little sister as well as she lost her child.

Richard, having an uncontrollable urge to just shake her out of her numbness, instead held her in his arms, comforting her and whispering in a soft tone to her, "You are still my little girl. Talk to Daddy. Please don't leave me like this, Marina, my baby. I love you so much. Talk to me."

His voice, always having a gentle, calming effect for her, awakened her, and she slowly came back to life.

Then turning toward him and with one word, she murmured, "Dad."

CHAPTER 16

Marina's existence traveled from the past, following like an arrow of time, shooting across the horizon, taking her in the direction of an unforeseen future.

Marina's life becomes like the sand in an hourglass, slowly as each grain passed, the tiny opening cultivated and sculpted her in the flow of time and into the inevitable.

Marina snuggled the squeezable pillow against her chest then stroked the soft fabric of the well-cushioned pale-blue sofa.

Inhaling the potpourri that drifted through the room, she spoke in a subtle tone, "I like the accent teal colors you chose for this room. I could fall asleep in this soft chair with the soothing aroma floating through this room." Marina yawned and stretched on her doctor's sofa.

Dr. Frances was not the typical psychiatrist. Her personality showed she was fond of joking to make her patients feel at ease, but her proficiency was defined by the core of psychological knowledge that skillfully helped her patients to surpass their depression and move into a new life.

Leaning back in her chair with her arms folded, Dr. Frances jokingly spoke with a twinkle in her eye, "Thank you, Marina. Are you just noticing my color scheme? We've been meeting more than a year. Or is this the other Marina I'm talking to?"

"Okay, Doctor, it's just me. I'm not running through a maze like a little mouse today. I seem to be enjoying the fact that I have you to talk to. My mind had vanished in a cloud of fog for so long, feeling like I spent all my life hiding my past. Now I feel like that bird outside your window—free."

"Thank you, Marina. I humbly accept your compliment and appreciate your change in observations. You have come a very long way this year and have become much stronger emotionally this last part of the year. When we first met, you suffered a long, abnormal condition of the mind. You now can differentiate what is real and what is false. Because of the sudden shock of finding your daughter after her death brought on an unusually delayed postpartum psychosis, usually that happens after birth, but for you, as we have discussed, it began again at her loss so many years later."

"Yes, Doctor, the hallucinations are gone. There was a time that my five senses were so alive about Cordelia. I don't see a physical Seton or hear her cries anymore. I know the medicine has helped a great deal and has allowed me to start a new life. All those bizarre ideas, like when you are dreaming but can't wake up, they have come to an end. Being rehired at The Post was a great happening for me. Everyone there greeted me and welcomed me back with such assurance."

"And Michael? I know he left and started his own practice back home in Tennessee. Since then, has he tried to contact you and resume your relationship?"

"Yes, Dr. Frances, we discussed our relationship, and it had to come to an end. I could not ever go back there again. Cordelia is there sleeping safely now. But our relationship and his parents have become strained. I just don't feel that my life can continue there. I love New York, and this is where my profession has led me."

"I am so proud of you, Marina. You have revisited your past traumas through your writing about your life. This manuscript has played a great role in your healing and will also in so many ways be a healing touch to those who have lived and lost in a way like you have. This will be a huge support and teaching to the women who have also had to undergo the same type of experience as you."

"Yes, I feel it has helped me to grow from grief to hope. Even though I can truthfully not make sense of what happened, yet in all the painful memories, I still feel that I moved forward and can look for good in my future."

"Marina, you have changed the face of secret adoptions and made it easier for those searching for answers to their questions. There will be no mystery in adoptions, but a solution for both parties with a common ground. Also, for the young girls that find themselves in an unexpected pregnancy, there is hope for them. I am in touch with a dear friend of mine. We have remained good friends since our college days. She is a retired journalist and now has a publishing company. When you are ready, I will send you to her, and she will guide you through the process. There is a whole new world waiting for you. Life is an unwritten book for all of us. You lived and now have written your untold story. Day by day and page by page you have designed a story worth telling. Enjoy your new life."

The next morning, Marina cleaned out her medicine cabinet when she came across the doctor's prescription bottles and noticed she skipped taking her medication for over three weeks.

She thought, *I don't think I need these any longer anyway. I'll just leave it in the back of this cabinet and won't tell the doctor. She didn't notice any mental changes in me during our sessions, so I'm sure I am mentally stable now. I feel great.*

Feeling a little tired, she decided to take a nap before meeting up with her cousin.

The same dreams returned each night: a child running through the grass, her eyes of liquid blue like the ocean so full of life, and her skin illuminated, running into her arms. Marina's fingers caught in her red curls as their heartbeats synchronized. There was a familiar scent filling her nostrils then slowly evaporating as the sound of her voice cried out in a loud shrill, "Seton," piercing like the crack of thunder splitting apart her dream.

She woke from her dream and realized she better get ready for her cousin's visit.

"Seems like we always end up talking in your room, Marina. The walls of this room hold all our laughter and our tears and all our memories."

"I know, Laurie. We grew up here. This was always our place to share. You're the best at keeping all my secrets, besides these walls. It's good to be back at The Post. I'm a step up from where I was more than a year ago, now editing for the chief and writing my own story. I never thought I would come this far, Laurie. I feel alive again."

"Dear cousin, how far are you in that book anyway? Seems like you have been so busy with writing I don't know how you make the time with your job."

Laurie was surrounded with colorful pillows propping her up as if she were sitting on a throne just like when they were teenagers.

"I stay up late and work on it. That's why you don't see me most of the weekends. I hide away in my room or at the library. My counselor said this has been the best therapy for me."

"Your parents are so happy in your progress, and I am so happy that this year has been triumphant in your career. Just think your name will be on your novel, and it's just one of many novels that you will be writing."

"Novels, my future fictitious narrative, but my first book will be one of realism, representing my life. Laurie, do you ever have dreams that are so vivid you think you are really there?"

"Not really. I think I dream in black and white, so boring. Why do you ask?"

"Oh, my dreams lately seem as if I am actually there. I found myself standing up when I woke!"

"Oh, Marina, my dramatic cousin, now you're sleepwalking!"

Their laughter blended into the room again as in the days of their teen years of sharing. It radiated outward into the apartment, bringing back the reminiscent of happy times.

The next day Marina received the phone call she was waiting for from the publisher her doctor knew and recommended for her novel.

"Marina, quick. There is a phone call for you. I think it's the publisher," said Margaret as she held the phone, covering the speaker with her hand, and with a motion of her head at Marina to move quickly.

"Hello, this is Marina. Oh yes, about my novel. Yes, I can tomorrow morning. Nine AM is fine. I will be there. I have your card,

Mrs. Clarke, from Dr. Frances, so I have your address. Thank you so much for calling."

As Marina hung up the phone, she wildly jumped on her mom, and they both hugged and jumped in excitement, falling onto her bed, laughing and giggling like two little schoolgirls.

It was early morning when she left for the IRT on Eighty-Sixth Street and Second Avenue, which was only a four-block walk from her home. The sky was clear and the air crisp as she joined the white-collar workers on their ride from uptown to midtown. Holding her manuscript tightly in its leather case with one arm and using her free hand to hold tightly onto the overhead holders, she breathed in a mixture of fresh, bathed commuters and some not in the habit of a shower.

I should have made a later appointment since this train ride will be for strap holders only, not one seat available, she thought.

Getting off at her stop at Times Square Station, she took a look at the card that Dr. Frances gave her, checking to see the address.

Marina thought, *This is an unusual name. Mrs. Eiluj G. Clarke? It seems to be a mix of a foreign name and a common American name. Well, I can't wait to meet her.*

Twisting her neck around to check which direction she went, she tapped her finger on her chin. She thought, *Umm, let me see. I got off the train on Forty-Second Street at Times Square Station, so I should walk one more block to East Forty-Third Street, then I'll look for building address number 132.*

Her eyes searched all the business signs, and she finally came to a stop as she found the matched address on the card. She thought, *New York Book Publisher, 132 East Forty-Third Street. This is it. Now I have to find the floor. Okay. Stay calm. It's suite 249.*

She felt her heart throbbing in her chest with anticipation of her first meeting with a publisher.

The elevator stopped on the second floor, and as the doors opened, she could see herself in the adjacent floor mirror. The lighting was a kind of brightness, like the fresh, new snow reflecting the sun. Racing down the hallway, she heard the echoes of her heels loudly clicking onto the marble flooring. *I wasn't expecting such an elaborate entrance to this office, especially in such an old building,* she thought.

She opened the first tempered glass door to be greeted by a young girl in her twenties, dressed very businesslike with a tailored black blazer, which brought out her sparkling green eyes.

"Hi, I'm Tina. Glad to meet you. How can I help you?"

"I have an appointment with Mrs. Clarke to review my manuscript."

"Yes, are you Marina? You're scheduled for 9:00 a.m., and you're very prompt. Follow me, I'll take you to Mrs. Clarke."

She followed through a pathway separating so many cubicles arranged down one of the hallways, and a wave of anxiety took over her feelings. Then straight ahead at the far end, she saw many massive offices lined up along a panoramic view of the city, but each one was separated by another wall of glass. The brightness of the sun shone through each office, giving such a warm feeling.

As she entered Mrs. Clarke's private office and was introduced, their eyes locked as she rose from her desk and gracefully reached out her hand to greet Marina. With a warm smile as illuminating as the sun, and her eyes flickering of blues, she motioned for Marina to take a seat. Not expecting to see such beauty, she appeared to be in her late forties and so youthful-looking with her soft, wavy red hair resting on her shoulders, Marina stared in awe.

"Thank you for sending your query letter. I must say, I became very interested in the first paragraph. I see the genre you picked is fictional, but I feel there are some truth hidden in between the lines. Could you emphasize a little more before I take the time to read your manuscript in full?"

Her voice captured Marina, bringing a trace of a memory, a vocal sound she heard before. Marina sat quietly, feeling like fading into the brightness of the room while her tongue asked for a drink of water.

"I believe we have reached the quality of life by our past uprising, which brought the liberation of women into our modern world. In comparison to the oppressed way of life before the 1950s, I took the lifestyle of young women repressed from the past and tried to bring these issues of abortion and adoption into public consciousness. This novel will bring direct awareness to the decisions we make affecting our lives. In this freedom of decision-making, is there a result or effect reached of either adoption or abortion. Does my story originate from my past? Well, that remains to be seen."

There was something puzzling in Mrs. Clarke's eyes as she listened to Marina's explanation while holding on to the query letter.

"Well, young lady, you convinced me. I'm very interested to read the remainder of your manuscript. Give me some time, and I will definitely get back to you. My colleagues and I will be meeting after I give them copies to read. I think this is a promising story."

That night Mrs. Clarke began reading the beginning of Marina's manuscript. As she read, it became like a photograph album, pictures flashing through her mind as she read of the lives of young women living through the difficulties of love and pregnancies from the early 1800s and onto modern times. The times and places where brought to life from across the world. She enjoyed how Marina combined the differences in culture and nations and yet how these women shared the same of young love and its difficulties.

She left the office early that evening with one thing on her mind—the picture hidden inside an old shoebox.

Her memories rose to the surface as she found herself fighting the timekeeper of life over the years. Her heart found some peace in the victory of success by hiding the truth deep inside her soul, never to let down the cloth of invisibility, her veil of secrecy. And then she met Mr. Clarke in college, and with his gentle manner and deep, trustworthy sensitivity that captured her heart and made it easy to unfold the secrets of her heart. He was confident in his work and led her to be strong, which she knew was an area of her personality that she needed.

"Hey, Mr. Clarke, are you home?" she said as she searched for her husband through the rooms of their huge center-hall colonial.

"Yes, Ellie, I'm by the pool."

She snuggled with him on his beach chair and squeezed his neck, afraid of letting go.

"You always call me Ellie," she said with a giggle, rubbing nose to nose.

"Well yeah, who could pronounce your real name?" he said with a wink of his eye.

"Oh, George, I had another bad moment today only because after reviewing someone's manuscript. It unearthed those terrible feelings I carry from what happened so many years ago," she humbly explained to her husband while still holding on to him tightly.

"I'm so sorry, Ellie. Do you think you should call your doctor for a time of counseling?"

"No, I just need you right now. You have been my box of secrets since we met. I'm so thankful for our marriage."

"I know, sweetie. It's been twenty years of a good, strong marriage, and we shared our secrets, which is why we are so strong together. I don't know what my life would have been without you."

"I believe it was fate that we met at journalism school. When I looked up and found you staring at me, I just melted. It was from that moment on that I fell in love, real love, for the first time."

"Yes, Ellie, all through college we were stitched at the hip. After we were dating for a while, and you showed me that you trusted me with your life story, I knew we would always have a good marriage. That's why I proposed so quickly. I didn't want to lose you."

"And I'll never forget the look on your face when I told you my real name—Julie Gagnon." She laughed heartily on his chest.

"Yeah, I just shook my head and thought, 'How in the world would she get the name Eiluj Gagnon?' Then when you wrote it backward to Julie, I fell in love with your mind also."

"Thank you for always listening to me about Cinderella. She will always be a part of my life."

"Ellie, she is a part of our lives together. And maybe someday in some special way we will actually find her. Why don't you spend time alone now? You know where you hide your secret letters and the picture you showed me."

"I was thinking the same thing. Will you cook dinner?"

"Of course, I already started a surprise recipe. And I think you need some privacy right now. Come into the kitchen whenever you are ready."

She knew he was right as she walked into their oversized bedroom with walk-in closets. She climbed up on the step stool to reach high above all the boxes they stored in their closet. She finally found the brown shoebox tied with a pink ribbon.

It's like a coffin, holding my painful memories of my child I will never meet, she thought.

She sat on the bed while opening it and waved away the dust accumulated since she last held it. Reaching through all the folded letters she wrote, she then found the faded picture.

She thought, *The pain comes back each time I look at you in this picture, Cinderella, but really the pain never leaves. It stays locked up in my heart. I was so young and innocent to what the world held at that time for me. You're so beautiful, and I have missed you all these years. Sadly, I will never be able to give you any of my love letters because I will never know where you are, and it has been years now. I'm sure you have the best of life all these years. Just wanted to stop by and see you for a few minutes.*

Holding the picture and all the letters tightly to her chest, she rocked back and forth, singing a lullaby, soft and sweet, placing the picture closely on her heart. Waterfalls emerged from her eyes with loud sobs echoing through the house.

God gave you to me, and I gave you away. But I will always be your mother, and someday, maybe in heaven, we will meet, she thought.

CHAPTER 17

A few days later, she read through half the manuscript, and she and her colleagues decided to call Marina for a meeting. "Marina, hurry. This is a phone call for you. It's the publisher!" Her mother's hand trembled as she covered the receiver with her other hand, keeping out the sound. Marina, with anticipation and adrenaline coursing through her veins, grabbed the phone.

"Hello, Mrs. Clarke, this is Marina."

"Marina, I have read through half of your manuscript and shared with my colleagues, and we have come to the decision to accept your story and publish as a novel. I will send you the binding contract for your signature, or you can stop by and sign so we can get things moving."

"Oh, this is great. I will come to your office tomorrow. No problem at all. Thank you so much for accepting this. I have been working on this endlessly."

"Marina, what a story. You have a special style and technique of communicating your ideas, and with your creative language, your characters have come to life. Your novel is so filled with suspense I cannot wait to finish the remainder of the book. Even so, I couldn't wait to call you with the good news."

After Marina hung up the phone, she turned to her parents with eyes wide and smiles cracked across their faces. She screamed with joy as words of excitement leaped out of her mouth.

"I'm pinching myself to see if this is really happening."

Marina felt giddy with excitement and started running and shouting through their rooms.

"It happened, finally something good. My book was accepted. I have to call Laurie."

"Yes, tell them to come over, and we will celebrate."

Richard replied with a melodic voice, almost humming and feeling much taller as he stood with a straight back in proudness of the news.

Later that evening when Ellie arrived home, her husband anxiously waited for her. He had something very important to share with her. As she entered their den, she found him sitting in his leather chair with his feet resting on the footstool. He looked up at her with the manuscript in his hand and his eyeglasses in the other hand.

"Ellie, I hope you don't mind, but when I found the manuscript on your desk, after reading just a few pages, I became suspicious. I felt compelled with a sense of duty to you, with many questions rolling around in my mind. Since I am a retired criminal justice lawyer and now a private investigator, I had an intuition, a strange feeling in my bones. So I hope you don't mind that I took the liberty of investigating the author. With that said, please sit down. we have to talk, but listen to me first."

Ellie cast her tired eyes around the room then raised her head, expecting the worst information he could find.

"It's okay. I trust you with whatever you have to tell me."

She reached over and held on to his hand as he spoke, looking directly into her eyes.

"After my systematic inquiry about the author of her novel, I discovered some facts about her. She was born in Canada. Ellie, do you know what I'm talking about?"

Ellie felt her facial muscles tighten as she gripped her husband's hands.

"Ellie, listen to me. She was born at The Fold in Canada. Her real name is Cynthia. I mean, Cinderella Cynthia Gagnon."

Ellie's blue eyes stared into her husband's face as her heart fell silent. He lips could not move as if stuck underwater; everything moved slowly, and her body began shaking.

George quickly grabbed her and held her tightly to his chest, stroking her hair in comfort.

"Ellie, I am so sorry that I shocked you, but I had to tell you. Ellie, please listen to me."

All at once like a flash, she shook out the sudden shock and held on to her husband.

"OMG, no, this couldn't be. All the times we spoke about her novel, it was my daughter. How could I have not realized? She was there in my office. I reached out, fingers and hands touched, we shook hands, and we spoke on the phone. I did feel something deep in my soul, something that was once lingering, then a tiny flicker ignited, and I felt a connection, but I ignored it. I understand that time has changed our features so that neither of us was aware of the distinction between us. But she was right there again in my arms, and I didn't know it was her!"

Ellie roamed the room as if trying to find something, wringing her hands together and swiftly pacing the floor, forgetting where she was.

"Ellie, come sit down. I have copies of the actual birth certificate. Here, take a look with me."

She sat down, holding the papers and with a burst of tears and deep sobs as she held the document to her heart.

"Honey, we can still find her. We have all her information, let's get in touch with her parents, tell them everything. they can help. I do believe all this has happened to reunite you to your child. I'm sure her parents will understand."

Then as if she leaped in the air, with fingers in spasm, holding the papers, it was like every atom of her being began to scream.

"The book, the ending, it's all coming together now. Even though there are no dates of time written, and she changed the name of the home to The Rescue, it covered up the truth of The Fold. I know exactly where it is, and I remember the day I traveled with my parents. I wish they were still alive to see her."

For a fraction of a second, George's mind became numb, then with the corners of his mouth twitched upward, he connected to what she implied.

"What do you mean, the ending? I didn't get to read the entire manuscript, but do you mean she is there? What did she write, Ellie? Tell me."

"It was a little dark and bleak. She wrote as if under an overcast sky. I couldn't understand all of it, I didn't quite finish it, but it was as if she was relating to being one again with something of the deep blue. She wrote about listening to the cries of the seagulls. As I read it, a chill ran down my spine, and I was wondering what she was relating to."

"We need to refer to you with your real name, not just Eiluj, but Julie, and your maiden name, Gagnon, if we want to explain all this to her family. Hopefully, your daughter will be with her parents when we arrive. If not, they will come with us if we have to go to The Fold. We can bring the picture you stored away of her when she was born, and we will bring the original birth certificate. I also have a telephone number for a Richard and Margaret Martin. My buddies at the office were able to track down the address and phone number of the family. I do believe it is them."

"George, I don't know how I would get through this without you, and this address of where she has been living is right here in Manhattan. How could we have been so close yet so far? I will make the call right now!"

Within hours after the phone interaction, they reached the address George retrieved while investigating Marina. When Marina's mother opened the door and set eyes on Julie, a flood of tears poured out. With a warm embrace, they held on to each other for a little longer, understanding each other's situation.

"Julie, this is like a forgotten dream. We often wondered what happened to the young girl who had to hand over her infant. We always thought of you with love and thankfulness that we were able to adopt and care for Marina, I mean, Cinderella. I am so happy to see that you have made a beautiful life for yourself. And you will be happy to know that Marina is a marvelous writer and holds a position at The Post. Oh, Julie, there is so much catching up to do," Margaret spoke with an unsteady voice as she held Julie, quivering slightly in their embrace.

"I remember that moment when I listened to the sound of your car drive away with my baby, but I was reassured that you would fill her life with goodness," Julie replied with a delicate smile, exhibiting kindness.

They talked for hours, revealing so many truths that were sealed for so long, exchanging documents as Margaret shared photos of Marina growing up.

"I can't believe that I was a grandmother, and poor Marina had to live through her own child's death. All these wasted years have come to this? My brain can't comprehend all this information. I can't even remember how to breathe right now."

Julie sat as sorrow filled her heart, but there was still more room for love to be placed for Marina.

"Julie, I know about the novel only by her talking about it, but I don't know the actually writing. She wouldn't let me read the manuscript until it goes to print. She said she was going back to The Fold for an interview. I told her she should not give up her profession at The Post. But being a stubborn child, she insisted on being a counselor. I thought that was a little strange."

Margaret's hold on Julie's hands lingered as they continued to talk.

"I'm glad you gave me this information that Marina is at The Fold. We should all leave together and find her. This is a perfect opportunity for her to meet my husband and me, plus with you both there at The Fold, it will all be so much easier for her. I don't want to call ahead because I don't want any interruption in our meeting. I think once she receives the proper explanation and the cause of my situation why I gave her up, she will understand."

Richard came over to sit next to Julie and, with compassion, gave her a hug, then he turned to George, and they had a strong handshake and then embraced then talked about the plan to leave for the fold.

"We will leave with you tomorrow morning. This is something that needs to be taken care of right now. She will be in shock again since the findings of Seton, but I believe she will rejoice when she finally gets to meet her biological mother. And then we will all celebrate together when this is over."

The next early morning sunrays were like a blessing for them as all four were ready for their road trip to Nova Scotia; they were devoted to emotionally supporting each other, which made the long travel easier for them all.

Each twist and turn of the country roads reflected the memories of so many years past, each one of them living in their own private thoughts of the past travel to The Fold and yet sharing in the same memory of going forward.

Julie sat by her husband as he drove, staring out the window, watching the road, anticipating her first meeting with her daughter, and longing for that moment of truth for each other.

"This is like a funeral with an awakening of the dead. I never had the power to heal. Maybe this is my time. I have to see her. I have to hold her," said Julie.

Margaret, with her soft voice and gentle mannerisms, tried to bring comfort to Julie during their ride.

"Julie, love is a healing element to the mind and the heart. Yes, her life was long and hard, but once she meets you, I am sure she will feel the connection and understand. You both have so much to share and have lived an identical life. Although it maybe strange and unheard of, time and love has reunited you both."

George replied to try and help with the somberness he felt in the car ride, "Well, I'm glad that you both are so kind and caring women. Also, Rich and Margaret, you are our new family now. Once Marina meets my wife, Julie, that is, and her mother. And when The Fold sees you both together after all these years, they will be so surprised and thrilled for sure. This will be like a family reunion."

"Well-spoken, dear husband. I'm so happy that our family is about to grow. It has been just the two of us all these years. I suppose that, with our professions, it has kept us very busy."

Julie's soft, manicured hands glide over her husband's. caressing in warmth as he clasped her hands strongly like an athlete, and both had an easy smile, acknowledging their anchored love.

Margaret reminded Julie of their visit to The Fold with Marina from a few years ago.

"Yes, The Fold will be so surprised to see you Julie. After we visited them with Marina when she found out about her adoption, she inquired about you. The director, Ms. Stella, remembered you and explained so much to her."

Richard's eyes filled, and he watched the farms he passed with his daughter and the calmness it brought then and now.

"This is like a time travel. A few years ago on this road, we all traveled at different times, and now in a few minutes, we travel the same road together for the last time."

CHAPTER 18

Marina made herself ready to meet with the director, for she cautiously planned a journey for her life. She had a hidden destination in mind. She thought of it as a beautiful beginning to a beautiful ending.

The director sat behind her desk, and with Marina's résumé in her hand, she reviewed her résumé. Then with her arms folded tightly over her freshly white uniform and with questionable eyes, she began to quiz Marina.

"I was surprised to receive your phone call, Marina, and happy at that, so you would like to interview as my assistant. How in the world did you hear of it?"

Marina sat across the desk with eyes glaring and fixed, as if they rusted into her sockets. Her stare wasn't intentional but cold and lacked a soft mobility.

"I was looking for something different other than my work at The Post when I started looking under assistant positions. It's definitely fate that I could come across The Fold needing an assistant!"

"Yes, this is divine providence. Your life mapped out from the time you were delivered here and then again when you arrived here as a teenager and now your return in a professional sense. I see you have acquired much experience written here in your résumé. I'm very impressed and proud of you. You have had a long life for a young girl."

"I want more in my life. What matters to me now is people's existence, the young girls who live here. That's where my experiences in life can encourage and help them grow into a new successful life for when they leave here."

The director sat back in her old leather office chair, folding her hands onto her lap with an uncertain feeling.

"We could use your skills and knowledge in this field. We had to expand the building due to the influx of young girls arriving here yearly. As you see, I have also aged over the years and am in much need of a assistance to relieve the excess intake in this facility."

"Yes, I can see the appearance of this building has changed a little. The Fold is renowned for its tradition and has earned its reputation by numerous works with those who seek refuge here. This place gives hope of a great future for the mothers and adoptive babies. The antique collectables here are glorious, adding charm and a glimmer of past cultures."

Marina talked a little nervously as her hands moved swiftly in movement with her words.

"Marina, you look a little pale, and there is a nervousness that doesn't become you. There seems to be a shadow over you. I remember your personality as a teenager. Is there anything else you would want to talk about?"

"Oh, it's just the excitement of it all and the presence in this old place. All the memories stored here are awakened by the surrounding waters sending in a scent of its own."

"Yes, Marina, that familiar scent. I understand that is why I just can't leave here. Even when I retire, I will remain with The Fold. Well, before we all make a final decision, you are welcomed to stay in our guest room just down the corridor, facing the south side. It's just a step onto the veranda. It's a little private there. Stay as long as you like. Come into the dining hall for dinner and meet the girls. Tomorrow is another day, and we can finish up our interview and settle it."

"Thank you, Director. I think I will take you up on that. I'll sleep a little since it was a long trip. Do you think it is possible to see my old room?"

"Oh, I forgot about the room you lived in while you were here. Actually, as you remember, it is upstairs, second floor, and has not been used for a year. We clean all the rooms weekly if used or not. So yes, you can stay there if you please. Are you sure you are up to that?"

"Oh, for sure, Director. It's been so many years. It would be fine."

"All right, Marina, go ahead to that room. Just be sure to come down for dinner to meet the girls."

Ascending to the second floor, her memory resurfaced of the last two morbid walks after leaving behind what she loved the most. This third and final time she remembered the feel of the old bannister as it arched under her hand. It had the same smoothness of oak as before on her last morbid walk up to her room. Then she heard a sound luring her into the room. An unknown language summoned her upward—a characteristic cry of a bird or a baby, like the sound of a distressed infant—but as she opened the door, it abruptly stopped. There was silence. A scent of the sea mingled with a scent of baby, like a breath landed on her face. There was no light that came from the window; it was like a seclusion room. There was no mark of time; the room remained the same, taking the air from her lungs. She sat on the bed, remembering her last time there, as she lay with an empty heart with just a small picture of Seton on her breast.

There was coldness like a draft coming from the one window in the room as a small ray peeked through, revealing specks of dust swirling in the white beams of sunlight flashing through the hundred-year-old window.

"The dust only shows me where my heart has been buried all these years, covered in its specs. An abandoned room since I left, I must have been the last young girl since Julie. This was her room. I can sense her presence here with the memories of my birth and of Seton. We both shared our joy and loss in this room. Strong beneath the dusty flakes of years. How vivid the picture of our lives remains here, Yet so empty. Even the scent of birth is gone. I can hear the scream of pain from Julie and myself."

That following morning at The Fold, Marina just woke from getting a few hours of rest from a sleepless night. Waking up was no longer a pleasure for Marina; her sleep was always violently woken like the sound of wailing sirens. For a fleeting moment, she still felt the heaviness in her arms and a faint vision of Seton.

Her head slumped into her hands for an immeasurable time and gave a sigh of satisfaction, knowing her true story was now written as a novel will be published. Physically and mentally tired with the shackles of internal grief buried deep and like a carousel of confusion in her mind, she knew she revealed her tragic truth that had been written in the last chapter of her book.

Marina thought, *I have been away a long time from a place where I first found what it's like to truly love. That life was really never behind me, but always inside the chamber of my heart. I secretly struggle behind what my doctor calls my beautiful smile. She doesn't know. The world doesn't know. No one sees my pain.*

She hurried downstairs to meet everyone for breakfast in the oversized dining room. She watched as each pregnant girl exchanged their feelings and remembered how she felt while carrying her child and living at The Fold.

"Hi, Marina, my name is Christine. I am so happy to meet you. I didn't get a chance to talk to you last night with everyone around and asking so many questions. But I just wanted you to know how impressed I am with your success. It gives us all inspiration that we will all be able to move on with our lives once we are done here."

"Oh, thank you, Christine, and thank you all. This is a beautiful place, not just physically quaint, but beautiful in the way of becoming comfortable while transitioning into leaving and beginning your new life."

The day went quickly with all the events that took place, and Marina became exhausted with each one she participated in. She finally had some time to be alone and decided to walk again to the sea.

She thought, *I hear the seagull cries calling me again. Do they remember me? Well then, I'll feed them the crumbs as I used to do whenever I came here to sit. I feel exhausted again. I think I'll just go back to my room. The infant scent lingers there and comforts me.*

She lifted herself step-by-step, thinking about her stay a long time ago in her old room, steadily holding on to the old oak banister, remembering how she had to walk down, holding Seton to give her away. She was awakened by the echoes of memories as she walked down the long corridor to her room. As she opened the door, the feeling of passing through an icy shower stung her. Sitting on the bed, her eyes caught the colors of the faded lilac and pink as when she first arrived. She pulled out the undetected old picture, which she wore daily, inside her blouse. She cradled it in her arms as a formless but distinct baby.

All these memories still fill this room, the same as the first time you were taken away from me, and then the tragic moment I found you for only a short time, a second time, a second death, she thought.

Her body jarred like a hard, physical blow searing through her; the air around her gave a hint of dead seaweed, and it was nearing into the darkness of night.

It took a very long time to say goodbye to you the second time, like a second death for me. Why do I still hear your cries? Is there a third death? Those never-ending echoing cries in my head, calling me, you're still alive here in my arms. Your skin is so soft, little one. We never left each other, Marina thought.

There was a chill in the air as she walked through the sea mist down the same path as she had before, walking into the limitless darkness. There was no struggle, just the sound of music and a lullaby.

Listen, Seton, as I sing you this gentle song. Don't fall asleep yet. Let me gaze into your eyes. Don't cry. we are finally together again. I waited so long to hold you. Let me enjoy this time with you, she thought.

Her mind lay dormant of that night Cordelia was lowered into the hungry earth. As the rain hammered the ground, she heard the earth groan again, wanting to be fed; with slight remembrances this time, she bellowed down into the sandy earth.

Watching the foam reflecting the starlight above, she tasted it over her lips.

She felt no fear as her eyes wondered far into the horizon. The tide with its ebb and flow changing into rolling waves and calling her with its menacing torment, enticing her to a watery grave as her heartbeat found synchrony with the waves.

"No, not this time. You will not have her. She belongs with me, here in my arms. We belong together, and we belong to the blue sea. This is where we have come into being. This was our beginning. It is our new dawn, and it is our fate," she said.

She already knew of her impending state as thunder rumbled and a bolt of lightning cracked the midnight sky.

"I was born at midnight. It's almost time to be reborn with you again, Seton, now at midnight. It's our only escape."

The waves formed arch-shaped hands, beckoning her with the strength of wild horses and the pounding of white foam as hooves. As the waves crashed against the boulders, the wind became stronger; baby cries grew louder, ringing in her head as this presence grew heavy in her arms.

"Seton, I'm sorry I left you once. I'll never leave you again. We will always be together now. Listen to the seagulls' cries. They are guiding us and singing you a lullaby."

The seagulls' tenacious cries grew louder, blending with the baby's cries, flying overhead in their winged flight, swooping in frenzied dives, and warning of impending danger.

All her thoughts were taken away, while her eyes were fixed steady in the bend of her arm. Her shoulders bowed over with heaviness as she carefully carried a weight in her arms, and her lips kissed each wave as if comforting her baby. The darkness of the sea did not threaten to swallow her, but bring her deeper to her peaceful destiny as the last current takes hold of her last breath. Streams of bubbles rose to the top as her feet touched the ocean floor. Her hair rose upward, and seaweed caressed her body, drifting around her head, crowning her Princess Cinderella as the cold water rushed inward.

The winds promised nothing but darkness as she rendered herself helpless beneath the sea. Midnight fell, draining the stars into nonexistence. Once it was a time of new beginnings and a new day, now it was her time of being born anew in her time of death.

Morning clouds kissed the brilliant sun, chasing away the leftover darkness and rain.

The sea was quenched as it gave her up to the sandy shoreline after taking her soul.

It took the medical examiner a few minutes to gather his thoughts and continue to examine her body at the sight of Marina lying there in the cool, wet sand. With her arms crossed over her chest as if holding her heart, her skin was still in a glow.

"I have never in all my days as a medical examiner ever seen seaweed so perfectly formed. It resembles a crown upon her head."

Julie, with a howling pain that tore through her, knelt before her daughter, lifting the soft, wet seaweed; then she lay down next to her, hoping to feel the heartbeat she once knew, but instead felt the wet sand beneath, as a small ripple of tides rolled upon them. She wrapped her arms around her daughter, feeling the return of cold caresses from her body. Tears distorted her vision when she felt something, like a stone or pebble, on Marina's chest. Lifting it out from beneath her shirt, she found a crumbled photo drenched with the smell of the sea.

"It's a picture of her holding her daughter. She carried it with her as if she were alive. OMG, I have the same picture of her in my arms at her birth. Now after all these years, I hold her again a final time. My Marina, you carried this hidden veil all this time for me and for your daughter."

She was crippled with pain and lost perception of where she was. Surrounding sounds of chatting disappeared as she held on to her daughter, searching into her eyes.

"Look how delicately this soft seaweed is draped around your face like a veil, just as you named your novel, *Veil of Secrecy*. My Cinderella, the pain is now over for you. But I now begin to bear the pain for losing you. Rest sweetly with Seton."

Her husband could not pull her away; the medical examiner and a team from the hospital could not interrupt this reunion in death. It ripped away not part of her, but the part she loved most—Cinderella.

The rain hammered as before, and the earth cried with hunger pains as Marina's body was lowered to join Seton's resting place. The veil of secrecy existed no more.

Julie's notes to Cinderella:

Today was a turbulent day for me, I found out I was
carrying you, I so want to keep you, but everyone around
me wants me to give you up. I want to keep you.

Your growing quickly inside me, I can almost hear you
breathe, I love the way you move around, and I love you.

I often wonder what you look like, your precious
little face, your little fingers and toes, I can feel you
playing inside, I can't wait to look at you.

*I was young, my heart taken by him and then left alone. As you
grew inside me, I was not alone anymore until that day you
were taken away from me, then and now I remain alone.*

What a beautiful sight, watching the snow falling; reminds me
of a lullaby I could sing to my infant. In just a few more weeks
into January, and I'll see my baby. Even for just a moment or
a day, to hold and then say goodbye until I see her again.

*When you were taken out of my life, your soul remained a part of me,
my dreams of you will bleed like a never-ending river, yet mended
by the visual memory of you, held in the basin of my heart forever.*

It's almost Christmas, so many gifts under the tree, but one is missing.

*Little child, I will give birth soon, I'll hold you then give you
away, I pray you get all the real love and attention you deserve.*

*You must be celebrating each birthday as each year passes,
I rejoice with you even though I'm not there with you.*

I have all my love notes to you hidden in a box
with your very first picture at the bottom,
Someday I'll share it with you.

One night in my dreams, you became so real to me again.

I feel so much life inside me; it is you my beautiful baby.

To feel life is to know real life.

So much had been created in this world, and I created you.

I closed my heart after you were born, drowning in a sea
of infinite isolation, but my never-ending notes to you
will remain folded away; because you were taken away;
my heart will not be filled until we meet again.

The sea brought you to me.
I loved you the moment I heard the news.
My secret cry flows to you, and we will meet again.
I can still see you when I walk to the sea.
Today would have been your first birthday;
you must be walking by now.
I can still feel your heartbeat. Can you hear mine?

My Cinderella, please forgive me.

Marina's notes to Seaton:

My sweet baby, I have no choice by to hand you over to another family. I pray they give you all the love you truly deserve. My heart will always ach for you but I believe someday I will see you again.

What a beautiful sight and just a few more weeks into January and I'll see my baby. Even for just a moment or a day to hold and then say goodbye until I see her again.

I was young and innocent, but I still wanted you, I would have done anything to keep you, I love you so much.

I closed my heart after you were born, drowning in a sea of infinite isolation, but my never-ending notes to you will remain folded away, because you were taken away, my heart will not be filled until we meet again.

The Sea brought you to me Seton, your name means from the sea, where you were born, but our secret is spell it backwards it becomes notes!

*I loved you the moment I heard the news.
My secret cry flows to you, and we will meet again.
I can still see you when I walk to the Sea.
Today would have been your first birthday;
you must be walking by now.
I can still feel your heartbeat; can you hear mine.*

I felt you in my dreams last night, your fragrance was all around me, and my hands went through your red curls. You must resemble me. I miss you.

Years have passed by so quickly; I feel that our time has come for us to meet, I just do not know when or how this will happen.
Dear Seton: Please forgive me.

ABOUT THE AUTHOR

Margaret Franceschini's desire to write in a dramatic way began at a young age. Her passion for poetry and short stories can be traced back to early childhood when she wrote about the creatures she watched in her backyard. Entering into adult life led her to join poetry sites, where she was able to share her innermost feelings with those of the same type of writings.

Later in life, she became intrigued with children of autism as she worked best with this population. Earning her credits with college writing, her essays always composed with her daily observation of their progression.

Through the years, she found the path to sincere friendships. While forming these friendships, she was able to gain trust and give them emotional support. They shared the trials of young love and the conflicting decisions of their pregnancies. Weighing heavy on their hearts with this dilemma, and abandoned by the father, left them alone, with a decision of either abortion versus adoption.

My story is a portrayal of young women from any generation that had to make a life-changing decision that, either way has remained etched in their hearts for a lifetime.